*Novels by Rick DeMarinis*

*A Lovely Monster* (1975)

*Scimitar* (1977)

*Cinder* (1978)

# CINDER

# Rick DeMarinis

Farrar · Straus · Giroux

New York

CINDER

CINDER

CINDER

CINDER

CINDER

Copyright © 1978 by Rick DeMarinis
All rights reserved
Published simultaneously in Canada by
McGraw-Hill Ryerson Ltd., Toronto
Printed in the United States of America
Designed by Cynthia Krupat
First edition, 1978
Library of Congress Cataloging in Publication Data
DeMarinis, Rick / Cinder
I.  Title   PZ4.D3742Ci   [PS3554.E4554]   813'.5'4   78–6739

*My thanks to the National Endowment for the Arts,*
*whose gift of time made this measurably*
*easier to write*

CINDER

INTEROFFICE MEMO
TO: *Weldon*
FROM: *Vi*
RE: *Mr. Cinder (see encl.)*

This is going to kill you, Weldon. The little notebooks he
wrote in were sent to the incinerator by one of the orderlies
after the old man's daughter, Mrs. Nettles, said she didn't
want to take them back to Minneapolis with her. She thumbed
through every last one of them, though—looking for cash, I
think—but she seemed embarrassed by what she found written there. Then there was the collection of wine bottles, empty
and otherwise, in his dresser. That really bothered her. Senile
is bad enough, but here he was a lush too. Poor girl couldn't
get back to the airport fast enough with her inheritance. Anyway, I'm glad I retrieved them, the notebooks I mean, from the
clean-up detail. I squandered most of Monday morning reading them. Weldon, they are cute! I took the liberty of having
Rita type them up for you, as the old man's handwriting was a
bit spidery. I think you'll get a laugh out of them. You just
never know, do you. I mean, about these old boys. I wouldn't

have dreamed in a million years that such a quiet little old gentleman was such a randy bedbug! When they go, they really go. Never a peep out of him, sitting there propped up on his pillows in bed filling these notebooks with his nutty ideas. He was always trying to con me out of a freebie peristaltic massage. A lot of the old boys do that. They like Nurse's hands. (By the way, Weldon, I never never came *close* to his miserable little pickle!) He'd gotten himself a bottle of Kaopectate just to make sure he'd get stopped up. But, other than that, he was one of our least bothersome patients. I think he was dead half a day before anyone noticed. Usually they're able to put up some kind of untidy ruckus to let the staff in on the occasion. Not Mr. Cinder. He went out quiet as a bulb. I hope you don't mind my using Rita. She doesn't have that much to do anyway. And we all need a laugh now and then, don't we? Especially our overworked boss, meaning yourself, Weldon.

Tonight?

This is the first of a bunch of notebooks. They hold an old man's story. I won't name it, for I can't think of a name that would cover all what happens in it. I'll just say that it is

*A True Telling*

You can take that for a title if you want, but it's not important.

They say truth always lies at the well's bottom. I don't claim to have gone that deep. I doubt if any man has. But I went down and stayed there until I had to come up for air. There's no point in drowning yourself for the arguable notion that there *is* a bottom or that it can be reached. But this is what they used to call, back in the seventh grade, a "figure of speech." This story hasn't got anything to do with wells.

*Ulysses Cinder*

*I don't know* who you are and you don't know who I am but if that's going to matter then you'd better quit now, for what I have in mind to tell you won't be easy to swallow even if you are inclined to take the word of a stranger. Someone here told me I was a senile wino. You can believe that if you want to. I don't claim to be as sharp as I was ten or twenty years ago. You probably aren't either. But one thing I am not, and that is a wino. Maybe you've heard them snicker. All right, so I drink the stuff. That doesn't mean a thing. Because a wino is a *bum*.

I was never a bum. I was never dirt poor. Money has always come in. I get my Social Security and a little more from a private pension plan I started years ago when I was still in the orange-growing business. There's a small nest egg over in the San Soledad branch of the First National Bank. Interest has been piling up. I don't draw on the principal.

I was married for more than twenty-five years. I have a grown daughter and two grandchildren who know my name. Before I moved into this place, I used to visit my wife's stone once a month with flowers. Roses. Yellows, reds, pinks, whites, what have you. I write letters now and then and get mail myself. And not just on Christmas. I have two blue suits and one brown and three pairs of good shoes. I always kept myself clean and had contempt for those who didn't. Now: is that the degenerate life of a wino? A fair man will say no.

I don't think anybody is reading this, which is probably just as well. I'm doing it for me anyway, and not for you. But if there is somebody reading along I want to let you know that what I am going to be telling you is a little off-base. That's why I started off with my wine drinking. To get that settled first. Anyway, no one could get drunk enough to make up from scratch all of what happened to me before I moved into this place. But if there are human eyes on this page, they are welcome. Old age does not rule out a man's need for company. I said I was doing this for me and not for you, but if you are reading with an open mind, then I guess I'm doing it for you too. I don't know how long it's going to take or how either one of us is going to make sense out of it, but we'll go through it together like a hike in the dark, one foot at a time, slowly.

Now: I did happen to sleep outside after putting away a considerable quantity of wine on that particular night. But it was in the park, over by the zoo. You will seldom, if at all, find the true wino sleeping in such a well-patrolled place as that. The true wino stays out of John Law's reach if he can help it. The true wino keeps to the freight yards or to skid row, where he is welcome. Once he wanders out of his proper domain, he can expect the sap and manacle and a day or two without his precious swill, unless they have started serving sparkling rosé with meals in the county lockup.

I remember it as a warm night even for that time of year. I went out for a little walk. I had my thermos with me. (Does a wino carry a thermos full of two-dollar-a-quart Pink Chablis around with him? Any schoolchild will tell you: Look for a skinny brown sack twisted tight near the top and a sweet stink like cough syrup in the vicinity.) I found a comfortable place near some high oleander bushes. I wanted to be shielded from the glare of headlights coming up off the freeway that runs by the park, so I could watch the stars which were bright as the lights from some kind of aerial city. It was about midnight, I guess, and I'd already had a short bottle or two of that Pink Chablis while watching a TV play about all the fun that was to be had on a day-to-day basis during World War II. I was a Tech Sergeant in the Quartermaster Corps and saw duty in North Africa and Sicily and I missed all the high times and good laughs and the chesty WACs that were waiting for you around every corner with fun and games on their minds. Seems to me that most people over there at that time were lonely and scared and wanted nothing more than to get themselves home in one piece, but then maybe those TV people saw duty in a different theater of action, where such things were common. I'm not saying they're liars, because after what happened to me—which I'll get to shortly—I would not question them if they said that the whole war itself was just a pastime devised by the king of Arabia to entertain his one hundredth bride, who was hard to please.

So I just laid myself back and sipped from my thermos, watching the stars crawl west and thinking about life in general—what it's all about—the kind of thoughts you have when you're young and when you're old, but don't hold much interest for you when you're a hotshot in-between. I guess I just dozed off, and with the warmth of the night and, yes, with the *wine*, I soon was stone to the elements just as if I was home in my own bed.

Here, then, marks the beginning of my tale.

The next thing I knew—WHUMP!—a tree fell on me. This is what I believed. I woke up out of a dream. It was a dream of elephants. I'd never before had a dream about elephants. They were in full stampede and I was lying in their path. The sun was up and high enough to half blind me when I opened my eyes to make out what had fallen on me. I was still hearing elephants in full gallop. It was thick and heavy. I was afraid it had cracked my rib cage. I said Ouch, loud, or tried to, but I doubt if much air passed over my vocal cords. I sucked in some wind and tried to holler for help. Someone did walk up to me, but I guess he figured I was just a wino having a wino nightmare, and when I tried to explain to him that I wasn't, nothing came out of my mouth but loony squeaks and clicks that probably only served to confirm his suspicions about me. I tried to point at the tree that had fallen over and pinned me down, but the passer-by just sneered and shook his head in disgust—he was an office worker on a bicycle—and pedaled off into the important morning that was waiting for him. I'll tell you something: most people have forgotten the school rhyme that goes

> *Mutual aid in times of despair*
> *Will make this ugly world more fair*

—forgot it or flat don't give a ladylike turd for the good sense it holds.

Well, shit with it, them I mean, the delicate prissy lot.

Pardon me, but I still get mad thinking about people like that bike-riding office worker. The world has always been going to hell in a handcart, but now I think that it's on a sharp downhill grade picking up speed.

So there I was with this tree, or what I thought was a tree, laying on me. I'm not a burly man any more, though at one time I was somewhat burly, but even so I tried to heave the thing off me with whatever strength my arms still had, but no soap. I pushed until I thought I'd bust a vein in my head, and considering the outcome of things in general, maybe I did, but it didn't give an inch. One thing was sure, though: it wasn't a tree. Pushing on it proved that. It was smooth and warm, and while it was hard, it wasn't the ungiving hardness of wood. This gave me something to think about. I relaxed under it, knowing that getting all worked up over my predicament wasn't the most intelligent thing to do just then—my pump had been giving me some trouble lately—and I tried to take inventory as best I could of the damage it had done.

I guess I passed out, or maybe I just fell asleep again. I had a dream. Something latched on to me. I flew down a black hall. It was like a car ride down an unlit tunnel through a mountain, but I wasn't in anything like a car. I was just flying along down a hall. There was a light in it. A pinpoint. I headed for it. As I got closer to it, the hall started to open up. There was a generous blue sky overhead and big white birds hung like sky sails against green hills. It was a valley and the light came from across a river. Something about that river was familiar, like maybe it was the American River up north or the Russian River up farther north, or maybe the River of No Return, which is in Idaho, farther north still, and the gathering brightness was more than just sunlight. A loud blast from an air horn scared me and I woke up. The horn was from a truck on the freeway. The sun had gotten itself above the stand of eucalyptus trees on the park's east edge and was pouring straight into my face, making it hard to see anything. The freeway was roaring with cars and trucks, and the thing that had trapped me was being lifted off. I tried to slide out from under it fast, but I was so stiff from being in one position for so long, I couldn't move at all.

It didn't matter. The thing kept on rising away from me. Rising and then bending, like it was hinged. I took a deep breath, which made my ribs ache. With the sun still in my face I couldn't make out anything except that some things were dark and other things were bright. The thing that had been on me kept bending away until it was gone. And then from somewhere behind me I heard a noise. At first I thought it was one of the big animals in the zoo. But it didn't have any distance to it. It was close. It was a deep raspy groan. I got it into my head that a lion had jumped the wall and was now sitting behind me sunning itself and yawning, too filled up with the morning's horsemeat to think of a skinny old man who was mostly dry skin and gristle as breakfast. So I took care to roll over slow and easy, without making a lot of commotion, for what you don't want to do is antagonize a lion who has jumped a wall to sample freedom. When I got over on my side, though, I saw that it was no lion. It was half hidden under the oleander in a kind of dappled light, but I could see that it surely was no lion.

Maybe in the long run it would have been better if it had been a lion. By the long run I mean the string of my life to its threadbare end, and maybe then some. The long run means more than I'll be able to get to in this piece of writing. This story isn't going to have an end, because I don't know what the end is going to be yet, but when I do know, I'll be long past being able or willing to write about it, for then the scribbler will be scrubbed. If that makes it hard for you to keep on reading, then maybe you'd better put this down and switch on the TV.

For the only end you will get to see will be just me sitting here in this bed writing. (I'm not sick, I just like to write in bed.) If I was a real story writer, I guess I wouldn't confess that to you at this point of the proceedings. A real story writer would try to make you forget that the end is right here in the beginning, being saved for last. For when he puts pen to paper, everything that's going to happen has already happened. Unless he just makes up things as they pop into his head. But if that isn't a form of chicanery, then I don't know what is.

Anyway, if it *had* been a lion, I probably would have gotten my picture into the *Tribune* and a TV man would have come by my apartment to ask me how it felt to be so close to the perilous jaws of death. I would have been locally famous for a day or two. Maybe my picture would have appeared in the *National Enquirer* along with a picture of the lion. "Pensioner Subdues Escaped Lion." That wouldn't have been so bad if it turned out that way. But it was no lion. No lion at all. It was a man. A naked Mexican (I thought he was a Mexican at first because of his looks), but bigger than any Mexican I had ever laid eyes on (and I'd seen a lot of Mexicans— migrant workers—being in the orange-growing business all those years in North San Soledad County), a giant Mexican at that, who was seven feet tall if he was an inch (it turned out later that he was half a foot short of being eight feet tall), just laying there under that oleander bush like he'd been clubbed half to death and robbed of his clothes, groaning, "I find myself in evil case," something like that, kind of formal-sounding or educated, almost sissified, like the English way of talking, saying, "He, the Frenchman, has made a cat's paw of me, sir, and has sought to compass my ruin," highbrow gibberish like that and crazy as far as I could tell, coming from a giant Mexican, crazy enough to make me look around for my thermos, which still had a dollop or two of Pink Chablis in it.

I now saw that what I had believed to be a tree was only his arm. He'd raised it up off of me to cover his eyes with his hand, as though he had a terrible thumping hangover. I guess I'd fallen asleep next to him, or him next to me, I don't know who was there first, and that tree-trunk arm of his had flopped over as he started to wake up, half killing me in the process. The inconsiderate nature of the incident made me mad, sitting there, watching the big brown wino waking up out of his fortified muscatel nightmares. "You goddamned near busted my ribs, you goon," I says.

He took his hand away from his face and turned his head toward me. The flat look in his beady black eyes made me regret my sharp tongue. A cold empty look it was, the kind you tend to associate with remorseless killers or psychopaths, the people in this world who are capable of doing anything at all for little or no reason. I felt that in those eyes I had about as much dignity as a sow bug. That made me madder still, but I had enough sense this time to keep my yap shut. We just looked at each other for a while, him laying in the cool black dirt under the waxy green leaves of the oleander, me sitting on the grass. We sized each other up. He was about as ugly a man as I'd ever seen. His head had been shaved like an old-time convict's, and new hair was just starting to grow in, like he'd just been let out of the state pen a week ago, and the dome of his big round head was blue. His nose leaned out of his face like a ship's keel. It was a big curving blade of a nose with a few spikey black hairs growing near the tip. He had a big wide mouth with brownish, wine-stained teeth (now there's a telltale sign you can always use to spot a wino in an otherwise featureless crowd), and I could smell his breath from where I was sitting two or three yards away. It reeked of something like sulphur smoke, the rotten-egg stink you roll your car windows up against when driving through a paper-mill town, but even with your windows rolled up you can still taste the foulness poisoning your throat. This big Mex is a bad hombre, I told myself. But I was never one to court trouble. Never trouble trouble till trouble troubles you. A valuable piece of advice with a long history of pigheaded neglect. So I got to my feet, not without a little pain from every involved joint, and started home.

"Ah, my friend, wait," he says in a big booming voice that hits the back of my head like a stinking wind. "I am in sorry straits, as you can see, old fellow. I am in dire need of assistance."

I thought: Cinder, you tired sack of half-calcified manure, are you going to make like you didn't hear him and keep on walking, or are you going to answer this big Mex wino criminal goon? But a twinge of pain across my chest made my mind up for me. I had to sit down again to catch my breath. I picked a spot in the shade.

She's here, so it must be ten. Vi Honeycutt, the day nurse. I'll get back to my story in a few minutes. Vi Honeycutt is what we used to call a dairy farm. By we, I mean the young boys of my day. Vi moves among the old men like a fine heifer among dried-out cornstalks. Old men rustle. They do. They are dry down to the bone. Vi will walk through the rec room and you can hear a crackling in the air. It's the dry old men rustling.

She's gone. Every morning at ten, she comes in wanting to know how I feel, and have I moved my bowels yet. Sometimes I'll lie to her. If I say no, then she gives me a peristaltic massage. But just now I didn't have to lie. I said, "Nope, not yet, Miss Honeycutt."

She said, "Not since yesterday?"

I said, "And even then, it was only a pellet."

"How picturesque, Mr. Cinder," she said.

This is all in fun. We get along just fine.

Then she pulled down the covers and went to work. She starts high up on the belly and works down, using only her right hand. With her left hand she holds up the back of my head.

"We need to activate the peristaltic reflex, Mr. Cinder," she said. "We want the large intestine to contract and work the waste materials down toward the rectum."

She has one of those low husky voices, and even though she was only talking about the intestines and such, she made it sound interesting. "There," she said, giving me a big wink. "That should get things started for us."

All the old fools in this place are hot for her. I saw a fight break out between two eighty-year-old bucks. They stood toe to toe and threw roundhouse haymakers that landed with the force of fluff. Like they say,

> A *woman's jars*
> *Breed a man's wars*

and Vi Honeycutt has the jars.

Anyway, this big Mex gets to his feet and walks over to me. He says, "Ah, good," thinking, I guess, that I had changed my mind about helping him out. "I am considerably in your debt, sir." He was grinning like a tickled ape. Now there was a sight for you. This giant wetback was covered with gray dust and a mulch of damp leaves and twigs, as though he'd been lying there out in the weather for a month and had become part shrubbery in that time. He was naked as day one and wide as two average men. I guess he must have been a good three hundred pounds, and that is probably a hundred short of the truth. I didn't have anything to say to him and my chest hurt like hammering hell, so I just sat there and stared up at him. I noticed something else, though, besides his size and mud-caked nudity. There was something in his ugly face above and beyond the sourness of a cheap wine hangover. It's not enough to say he was down in the dumps with a skull-cracking bun on. It was more than that, and surprising to see in a fierce unholy map like his. He was sick with some kind of grief. Grief. I recognize grief when I see it, because I have seen it more than once in the mirror. But his wasn't exactly the same kind. This is hard to explain properly. I mean, it wasn't *personal*. It wasn't like something terrible had happened to him yesterday or the day before, but something general and persistent and more or less incurable. It was like he was born with that look on his face. And the big phony grin he wore just drove the point home. So did the shrewd gleam in his squinty eyes. That big pumpkin head had an unhappy mask carved on it, and the beady eyes and the toothy grin only added to the effect, even though it seemed that he meant them to accomplish the opposite. I'm trying to tell you how he looked to me on that first morning, but it's hard. Not because I don't remember, but because I don't have all the words I need.

(This tires me out. Not just the brain-busting I have to do to come up with the right words, but the effort of pushing this pencil across the paper, page after page. And then my thinking will get crossed up, too. Things come into my head, sometimes in threes. I want to set them all down at once because I might lose sight of them.)

Maybe this will help: He made me shiver even though the park that morning was warm. And I wasn't shivering because I was scared. I felt salt in my throat. I felt like I wanted to sneeze. The expression on his face did that.

You reach a point in your life when you figure you've just

about seen it all. The last time you were surprised by people and their antics is dim in your memory. The last thing to surprise me was the 1948 election. I was just a little more than forty years old at the time, but even at that age, the world can hold little shocks for you. A thing can come along and you're a greenhorn all over again. How did that little haberdasher get to be President? The whole country was asking itself that question. Pundits and dopes alike. I didn't think I could be hung up to dry by an unexpected event ever again, but I was wrong. I stood up. The top of my head was about even with a point midway between his elbow and shoulder. He reached out to shake my hand. I stuck my hand in his. It disappeared like a minnow in a whale. He didn't squeeze hard to impress me. I took my hand back. It was tingling warm, like I'd passed it over fire.

"Ulysses Cinder," I says. And he says his name is Sadass. I figured I misunderstood him (even though the name surely fit), because he'd hiccupped just before he said it. But I didn't ask him to repeat it, for when he opened his mouth his corrosive breath steamed out at me and one close-up exposure to that was enough. I turned to leave again. This time he put his hand on my shoulder. He didn't say anything. I kept moving and his hand slid off. My shoulder tingled where he'd touched it. I guess I was about fifty feet away when I stopped again and turned around. That aching sadass face was still grinning. He was in need. But I was in no position to help him. Not out of the hole he seemed to be in. Even so, I hated to see a man so down and out he couldn't even cover his misery in rags. So I shrugged and walked back to him. "All right," I says. "You stay here, under that bush, so no one will catch sight of you. I'll go down to the Salvation Army store and get you a coat or something. You can't run around San Soledad like that, for the police here can't stand the sight of blemishes. It isn't good for the tourist industry." He grabbed my hand and started pumping it to beat hell. "Hold off," I says. "Don't get any ideas. I'll get you a coat, but that's going to be it. You're on your own after that." His smile got bigger and he crouched down slowly, backing into the shrubbery until all you could see of him was the round shadow of his big head and the black unholy glint of his eyes.

There was one of those new half-size commuter buses that stopped every twenty minutes at the park and went all the way down to the waterfront and then back out to the east valleys. I got on and rode it as far as Pizarro Plaza in down-town San Soledad, where I got off. The Salvation Army store is about four blocks south of the plaza on the edge of skid row, and it was not a favorite place of mine to loiter in. I hurried through the racks of coats, trying not to pay any attention to the winos and the poverty-row people who were also shopping for bargains. I picked out the biggest piece of material I could find. It was an army overcoat, a class-A full-dress heavyweight coat the size of a pup tent, with top-kick stripes still on the sleeves, along with hash marks indicating thirty years of honorable service. I paid two dollars for it and took the bus back to the park, ignoring the stares of the winos and the Bible-thumping street preachers in the plaza while I waited for the little Mercedes-Benz to arrive. Sadass was still there under the oleander bush. I was half sorry to see that he was, for I still had misgivings about his intentions. The coat almost fit him across the shoulders, but it was short. The arms of the coat stopped six inches below his elbows. The bottom of the coat stopped above his knees. He buttoned three but-tons and stepped out of the bush and into the sunlight, the damndest top-kick any army has ever seen. I stuck a dollar into one of the coat's pockets. "That's all I can do for you, Sadass or whatever," I says. "It isn't much, but maybe you can get back to your people now."

I turned away from him, thinking: What people? What people would claim him? But I felt better for having helped him. I'm not a religious man, but I believe this much is true: kings and cabbages go back to compost, but good deeds stay green forever. Under the skin we are all related, and the common ground of blood, bone, and meat makes us charter members of the same humble club, say what you will about superficial differences. Yes, I am a democrat, in spite of what you might have heard about orange growers, for in my book no man stands alone unless he stands on the broken dreams of others.

But when I got out to the sidewalk he was still with me, following about ten feet back. I didn't know it at first, but from the funny looks that began coming my way from other pedestrians and from the gawkers riding in cars and cabs, I figured something was going on behind me. I figured right. Sure enough, there he was. Grinning from ear to dirty ear, padding along in his mud-caked, size 22 feet, looking like he was fully equal to the sorriest piece of human wreckage the race has managed to produce in the last hundred centuries, and I regretted all at once having befriended him and was ashamed of my regret. It doesn't take a college professor to point out that

> *A kind gesture shown:*
> *A seed of trouble sown.*

But if you choose to live your life by that poor motto, your heart is destined to shrivel up like a little pea and your spiteful mind won't give you a minute's peace. Both ways are hard, and there's no other route. It's a fork in the road of life we all eventually come to. But the low road of cold indifference leads without fail to heartache past all the anodynes. The high road isn't any easier, but it leads to peace of mind. These are things the old need to think about. The young do, too, but for them it's not an urgent matter, for there is time to mend the mistakes of oversight and ignorance. So, as I saw it, I had a poor choice: get rid of him now once and for all or take him home for breakfast. I turned to face him one more time. I said, "If I flagged down a cop, you could get a meal in the city cafeteria." But his grin failed and the dark sorrows in his eyes got darker. So damn me for a softheaded fool if I didn't take him home to share my food.

How did I get to be such a fool? I don't know. I'm a fourth-generation American, born in the heart of the country, Tonganoxie, Kansas, in May of 1906. My dad was George Chester Cinder, and he was born in Defiance, Ohio, about 1878. My mother's name was Willa Tarmigan Benson, and she was born in Rome, New York, I forget the year. Dad was a locksmith. We moved on to Denver from Tonganoxie in 1925 and then to Salt Lake City just before the crash of '29. Dad wanted me to take up locksmithing because, in spite of the crash, he had established a good business in Mormon country and didn't want it to fall into a stranger's hands when he retired, and I did take it up, but it wasn't what I wanted to do with my life. So when the war began in earnest in 1942 I enlisted in the army, with a definite sense of guilty escape. Dad and Mother argued against it. So did my girl, Emily Jewel Noffsinger (who later became my wife), but I told them all it was only a matter of time before they started drafting men over the age of thirty-five and that if I went into the army before that time I might have some chance of picking out the kind of duty that suited me most. I didn't know if that was true or not (it turned out not to be, but by a happy stroke of Providence I landed in the Quartermaster Corps, which was a better place to be in the North African and European theaters of action than the front lines), and by 1945, when I came home, Dad had gotten himself an apprentice—Frank Cartwright—who was about as good a locksmith and as decent a man as there ever was west of Denver, and by 1946 Dad had made Frank a full partner. So when I told Dad that I was going to take Emily (my bride) to California to grow oranges in a little spot next to the Pacific Ocean, he didn't object but gave me his blessing instead, along with a check for one thousand dollars to get started on.

But that's the personal history of ten thousand other people, too, and it doesn't go very far toward an explanation of who Ulysses Cinder is or why he does the damn fool things he does.

So I let the big hobo into my clean apartment and fed him my food while my furniture buckled under his aromatic tonnage. And that's how it all began a while back, several months ago, once upon a time like they say in the story books, on that sunny morning in the park, take my word for it or call me a wino liar, it's purely up to you.

(That fills up my notebook. This one is shorter than the following ones will be, because it was hard to start. I tore out a bunch of pages. I thought it would be easy to put down, but it wasn't. Getting started took four pages. I lay here looking at page 1 for two hours. It was blank as a hospital wall and it wanted to stay that way. It was obstinate. It dared me to put something intelligent down on it. I struggled. I stabbed it in frustration, broke my pencil. I finally had to drink a pint of table wine to soften that paralysis of hand and brain. I feel sorry for real writers who have to do this sort of thing all the time or starve. But they're probably warped, anyway, as most people are who are attracted by strange and unnatural occupations.)

*Notebook 2.* Assad—that's what he said his name was, some kind of Arab name, but I tended not to believe it backwards or frontwards, as we don't have many Arabs in this part of the world. I fed him a plate of last night's spaghetti, cold, with some garlic sausage, hash browns, boiled eggs, biscuits, and he was still hungry and asking for more when it was gone. I made him six slices of toast, a bowl of oatmeal, and found a partly full week-old container of potato salad I had got at a delicatessen, but he loved it anyway, he loved it so much that he tore the container open and licked the paper clean. I hadn't gone grocery shopping for a while, and all I had to give him after that was a can of beans and a jar of sweet gherkins, but he didn't seem to mind, for he gobbled that, too. This is what happens when you start fancying yourself the Good Samaritan. It's easy to see why some people are cold fish all their lives, nursing a grievance against strangers.

He sat there at my table in his wool army coat picking his teeth with his fork and passing sour gas. He was sweating like he was in a hothouse. He didn't pay much attention to me, but when he did happen to look my way, he'd flash that phony smile like he was all so humbly in my debt or like I was some "Padron" (I'd seen the look back in my orange-growing days on the faces of wetbacks who were used to dealing with tyrant farmers in both countries), but he didn't want to pass the time of day in small talk and it seemed there was a lot on his mind. I knew by now he wasn't the simple goon I at first took him for when I saw him naked in the shrubbery, but I still didn't think much of him, and I guess no one would, considering his less than humble circumstances.

I showed him where the bathtub was and how it worked, in case he'd never seen one before. I showed him the mouthwash and how to use it, and gave him the box of kitchen detergent. I set my little TV set on the toilet seat to keep him company. I thought that if he got interested in some program he'd get a good long soak and maybe some of the crud would dissolve off his hide. Then I went out to see if I could find some clothes that would fit him. I headed for Goodwill, the big thrift store down by the beach. It was a short walk. The weather was just about perfect, temperature in the seventies and the sky blue as blue paint.

NUTS!!

Interruptions. Get going good and someone's got a question. That was Vi Honeycutt again. On her way to town. She was wearing slacks and a sweater instead of her white uniform. She's something. Wanted to know if she could pick up anything special for me. I said no. She hung around for a while, straightening my covers, adjusting furniture, neatening up in general. That plum-colored sweater of hers looked like it had twin speedboats in it with the handsome bows lifting up out of the water as the throttles of the big inboards are pulled out to all the way wide open, zoom. "Are we *sure*?" she said. "I'm sure," I said.

I'm just glad she didn't get a notion into her head to check my pulse. ("My, we are a thumping wonder, aren't we?")

As I walked toward the Goodwill store, I asked myself some pointed questions. Such as: What did I think I was doing taking in a bum? Not only that, but why was I spending considerable resources on the big wino? And not only that, but I had left him all alone in my apartment! That is a dumb thing to do. I might come back to find the place stripped to the walls and him long gone for the freight yards. I guess that would be a real worry under normal circumstances, but my true thinking behind this was that he might *never* leave. What could I do if he said, "You are the first decent old boy I have met in this scumbag town, and so I guess I will stay on for a while"? Befriend a rootless giant and you can expect the worst.

Goodwill had some outsize denim work pants and a lumberjack's shirt that looked like it would fit that friend of Paul Bunyan's called Johnny Inkslinger who Paul found one day scraping a limestone bluff with a jackknife the size of a four-horse doubletree, with the shavings flying like bullets over a mile away. I couldn't find a pair of shoes or boots that came close to matching his gunboats, but I did find a pair of huge Mexican sandals that must have been made as a joke by some shoemaker with a limited sense of humor. I bought the lot for five dollars. He wouldn't look like much, but at least he could walk down the street without getting himself arrested. Scrubbed up and dressed, he maybe could get on as a strongman or as a freak in some amusement park for room and board and I could close the book on this particular good deed and be done with it. As I watched the little hippie-type girl tie up my bundle with string, I had a strong and satisfying feeling of accomplishment. I'd done my part toward getting him back on his feet, now the rest was up to him. There are people who would call me a smug self-satisfied old man and there are others who would call me a sucker. But you're making a big mistake about this life if you think you can come out of it ahead of the pack by treating your neighbor as a grower might treat an infestation of whiteflies. Of course, I also knew that I was no Brother of Charity dedicated heart and mind to the welfare and betterment of my fellow man. But it was a pure and simple act of kindness and not an act of greed or meanness, and I think that will stand up to anyone's final accounting if it's at all fair and if they ever have one. Even so, I can hear the laughers now: he is old and afraid of dying and so he's catching up on his good deeds to beat hell, as if one or two paltry acts of common decency are going to make up for a lifetime of spite and indifference. All I can say to them is: You are wrong.

After Goodwill, I stopped at the delicatessen and bought another quart of potato salad, a pound of garlic sausage, and some cheese. I was winded by the time I got back to the apartment building, and the chest pain that had hit me earlier came back. Not as sharp, but deeper and more persistent. I had to sit down on the front steps for a couple of minutes until the bright spots in front of my eyes went away. Then I went up to my apartment.

Sadass (that's how I *heard* his name, even when he said it right, without hiccupping) was still in the tub. He'd made himself a bubble bath with the detergent. He was watching a soap opera called *The Secret Second World*. I often watch it myself. It was one of those offbeat soap operas where they have crazy people who see things that aren't there and good-looking female crime-busters who say things like, "Dammit, Fred, they are not going to 86 this caper after I have flaked my collar, are they?" I never know what's going on, but that doesn't interfere with my enjoyment of it. He also had my newspaper and a few magazines, and they were all wet. He had a brooding look on his face, as if he had been working out something in his head. His mouth was hanging open and he was frowning. He looked like an ape trying to add 2 and 2. He looked comical, the big rube, all accordioned up in that bathtub—which was big for me but bucket-size for him— with little puffs of detergent foam sitting on his upright knees, but I didn't interrupt him. I set the package of clothes down on the floor next to the toilet and went out to the kitchen, feeling all of a sudden like the biggest idiot God ever took the time to invent.

I fixed myself a sausage and spooned some potato salad onto a plate. It was a little after twelve noon, and I was hungry. The easiest way to get sick when you get to be my age is to start in skipping meals or to feed yourself poorly. Some people believe the old bogus saw that goes: Steal an old man's supper and you do him no wrong. But it is the worst piece of advice I have ever heard. If your grandpa starts missing his meals, then you can be sure he is on the unmistakable road to the bone yard. P.D.Q. Absolutely. I have seen it. Good solid food is important to both the young and the old. When you're a hotshot in-between, you can survive on crackers and beer and still dance all night.

The kitchen table in my old apartment sat next to a pair of French doors that opened out onto the street. I had a nice leisurely lunch just watching cars drift by. Some young people were milling around on the sidewalks. Kids, beach kids, with blond hair and brown skin, with nothing at all to do and not a bit worried about it. I don't mind them. I minded them when I first moved in, after Emily died, because of my poor frame of mind at the time, but I got over it. After I came out of that funk, my attitude changed. There are too many oldsters in this world whose main idea of intelligent conversation is the wholehearted enthusiastic criticism of the young. It's wrong. Whenever I run into one of these white-lipped jaspers,

I let him know right now that I am not going to help him pick bones. (I'm pleased to say that I have not run into very many of them here at Sunset Haciendas.) There is a time to be young and a time to be old and you don't get a second chance at anything, so you might as well enjoy life while you can and quit the excess griping. I guess you don't want me to preach at you. But it's just common sense.

By the time I finished my meal, it was going on one. It was a little early in the afternoon for the daily fortification, but I decided that there was something special about the occasion and opened up a corked bottle of Zinfandel. I guess I figured I'd earned myself a treat. This was the four-dollar-a-fifth variety of Zinfandel, straight from a small winery in Modesto. I poured myself a generous glass of it and went back to my street watching. A girl and a boy walked by holding hands and I raised my glass to them. They saw me and waved back. There wasn't a shadow of unhappiness on their brown faces and there probably never had been. They were a joyful pair and they believed their happy condition was permanent. They didn't know about how time changes things and that nobody can stand unbent before its tricky schemes. Time is, time was, and time will be, and that's that, nothing is going to change it. I took a drink. I sighed. I took another drink. I refilled my glass.

When Emily died, I sold the grove to a real-estate speculator who intended to put up a tract of small houses with no back yards, when the price was right. But I sold out because everything in our home that reminded me of her proved she was gone forever and it started to kill me inch by inch, for I loved her. I knew that if I stayed on, I'd be underground in a year myself, and I wasn't ready for that. So I took the apartment down in San Soledad on the old north side, not far from the park and only a stone's throw from the beach. A good location. You've got to make choices in this life, and some of them take gumption, but if you don't, the ground will surely reclaim you ahead of time, one way or another. There I go again, preaching. It's one of the afflictions of age. But that doesn't make what I'm saying wrong. Listen, you can't let sentiment fog your thinking. That's all I'm saying. If you expect to live out your three score ten, plus a few more than that, thanks to medical science, then you have got to get organized. Good food, a decent cheerful place to live, and the cultivation of salutary thoughts. Tea and toast and morbid notions: that is the quickest way to a one-room bungalow under the tulips.

Emily was only fifty-six when she died. She was never a robust woman to begin with, and I watched her waste away before my eyes. The doctor told her that her dizzy spells and faints were due to low blood pressure and a weaker than average heart action. From that day on, she led the life of a semi-invalid. From bed to couch, from couch to chair, from chair to bed, and you couldn't talk to her without bringing tears to her eyes. She grew thin and turned bone-white. Her hair went white and her pretty blue eyes got white and rheumy. It made me heartsick. I tried to get her to take walks down on the beach and let the sharp salt wind toughen and brown her skin, but she wouldn't leave her chair. I tried to give her eggs and red meat, but she wouldn't lift the fork. She would not budge out of her housebound routine. She'd sit there wearing a comforter, sipping sugared tea and nibbling toast and turning the pages of a magazine with weak fingers. You could see she was preoccupied with melancholy thoughts. It went on and on. I couldn't do a thing to stop it. At times I felt there was something deliberate in it and I got mad at her. (Later I found out I wasn't totally wrong.) I yelled at her once or twice when she wouldn't eat. But she was like a candle burned down to the holder and flickering. It was a hard time. I loved her. But she died anyway.

She never did have a hearty grip on life. She was a delicate woman who got more enjoyment out of a magazine or book than from a sunset or the coming in of a squall that would make the skinny palms along the Pacific Highway bend like they were made out of rubber. Things like that always interested me, but Emily was an indoor woman. She never took an interest in the health of the trees in our grove or in the size of the crop or worried like I did about vermin and frost. And when I told her that I often talked to my trees, sometimes for as long as an hour, she looked at me like she couldn't tell whether or not I was pulling her leg. Sometimes she would come out to help me carry the oil heaters during a January cold wave, but I always knew that she was doing it for me, not for the trees. If I talked about the knotty problems or strokes of blind luck or the swindles of the middle men or the roughshod methods of the big canneries, the things you encounter in the orange-growing business, she only pretended to be curious. But I could see it all bored her. She was a dreamer who didn't make strong attachments to the commonplace necessities that most people have to deal with. I believe she loved me in her way. I can say that now. But there was a lot about her I didn't know. I suppose there still is. I don't think anyone ever gets to know very much about anyone else, married or not. You think you know, but what you know is what you want to know. What you don't want to know makes itself known as irritating traits. It goes deeper, but you write it off as little peculiarities. Oh, there were times when her retiring nature irritated me no end. I often felt locked out of her thoughts. But I loved her just the same, and wrote her strangeness off. It's a common mistake with a guaranteed longevity, people being what they are.

I poured another glass of that good Zinfandel and took a peek into the bathroom. He—Sadass—was still in the tub watching TV, the afternoon news update, with the sopping *Tribune* spread over his knees. I started to tell him to be careful switching channels because he might electrocute himself, but thought better of it. If he was that dumb, then it was dumber of me to think that his survival was in my hands. He seemed about forty years old or more, and if all seven feet of him—actually it was seven and a half feet of him, because I had seen him graze the top of his head in the doorway coming in, and I knew that the clearance was exactly seven feet six—survived that long without getting electrocuted, I suppose he had something going for him that would pull him through this particular bubble bath.

Going back over these past few pages, I get the feeling that I am spending too much time on that morning I brought him home with me. Maybe so. But it seems right to go over the details. Like they say: first impressions are last impressions. That's not exactly the whole reason, though. Maybe you'll see later on why that first time in my apartment was so important. See, from that time on, nothing was the same. So it sticks in my mind. But if you're bored, skip ahead a few pages.

I gave myself another glass of wine, being careful by this time to not hit the rim, and then I went into the living room. There was a locked teakwood box I kept under the sofa. The key for it was behind a row of books on the built-in bookshelf. I'd never read a single one of those books all the way through. They belonged to the previous tenant, who had left them there when he moved out all at once in a big rush without even telling the landlady. His name was Ralph M. Dimsetter. All the books were stamped with his name, that's how I know what it was. There was a snapshot of him in one of the books. He's standing on the beach with a woman. They are wearing bathing suits that date back to the twenties or before. Behind them is a Model T, up to the wooden spokes in sand. They are a handsome couple and appear to have a close relationship to the photographer, because the expression on their faces is friendly and sort of indulgent, as though a beautiful child was taking the photo. Now why did I think that? But that's what I thought. Maybe it was their child. Maybe the child had never used the Kodak before, or was backward with mechanical things. I had to be wrong about that photo. Old Ralph lived here all alone, and when he left, he didn't take anything with him, like a fugitive from justice and not a family man at all.

One of his books was called *Myths and Legends of Flowers, Trees, Fruits, and Plants.* I once, just out of curiosity, looked up "The Orange," since a nice grove of them once provided me with a fair income for a number of years, but there wasn't anything of practical interest in what I read. Some nonsense about them being the golden apples of the sun in a place called the Hesperides and how some roughhouse goon called Hercules had to fight off a dragon to get himself a few. But it was behind this particular book that I kept the key to the teakwood box. I pulled the book out and felt for the key. It had been months since I'd used the key, and it seemed like now was as good a time as any to open the box and have a visit with what I'd come to think of as another key of sorts.

This other key is an old revolver that belonged to my dad. It's a long-barreled nickel-plated .38 caliber affair with fat cherrywood handles. There are bullets in the cylinder. I call it another sort of key for a special reason. I'll tell you about it. My dad died of a stomach cancer. It took him a good long while and the pain of it was too much for anyone to bear up under. So when he finally died, he was stark-staring crazy.

Shortly after that, Mother had a stroke. It left her without control of her lower body, including the organs of elimination, and by the time she died she was senile and had to be cared for in a home. All that Dad had saved went into that home, and to the doctors. Once in the home, all she ever talked about was how to fix turkey giblets, and nothing the doctors did could get her off the subject. I didn't expect any better treatment from the quirks and quacks of fate. No one should. These are the conditions of life these days. Like they say: life is an onion—as you peel it, you cry. But I figured that if I got just a little advance notice, then that's where Dad's big .38 would come in. While I still had a brain that could think and a hand that could move, I would personally open up the gates to the hereafter with that master key without thinking twice. That's the way I felt about it. I have since changed my mind for reasons I'll be getting to. I can hear you scoffing. Well, I know it sounds like easy brag, like the fella who said he was going to row across the Atlantic but changed his mind. But it isn't brag. I was serious.

I opened the box and took out the gun. It had never to my knowledge been fired. It was an old gun, a nineteenth-century piece, but it looked brand-new. It had a brass trigger and fancy scrollwork engraving running up the barrel. I picked it carefully out of the box and aimed it at the wall. The sight wouldn't settle on any one thing. That was because of my hand, which was somewhat shaky. Out in the street some kids were singing love songs and playing a guitar. I walked to the oval mirror hanging on the wall next to the bookshelf. I looked at myself. I saw how the gun looked held up against the thin bone of my gray temple. I did this fairly often. A kind of dress rehearsal. The shining gun looked fine and strong, and I looked old and worn out. I looked like a burden to myself.

Then all of a sudden a pair of words drifted in through my French doors. "Do it." I saw that there were tears rolling down my face. I saw my finger, bloodless-white on the brass trigger. The words were from the song the kids were singing. "Do it." The guitar seemed like it was in the room behind me. The girl singing had the voice of an angel. I guess I went a little crazy. When you get old, there are moments when the brain rearranges the proper spacing and ordering of things.

I stepped away from the mirror. I put the gun back into its box, put the box back under the sofa, dropped the key behind Ralph Dimsetter's useless book, but the stinging tears continued to seep out of my foolish old eyes. Well, maybe it was too early to start in on something as rich as four-dollar Zinfandel. I went to the sofa and laid down. I dozed right off. I had a dream. I was outside in the street with the singers and I was dancing as they played.

I woke up. Sadass, all dressed up in his new clothes and smelling of detergent and Listerine, was watching me. He was grinning. This time it didn't seem so phony. But then his expression changed back to sly and he said, "You have shown me great kindness with no hope of personal gain," just as phony baloney as ever, complete with English you would hear only in a movie about perfumed swordsmen.

I sat up. "A man wrapped up in himself makes a small package," I said.

He laughed. "You are a philosopher!" He had the bottle of Zinfandel I had emptied in his big hand and he was laughing at *me* as if he suddenly understood how big a soak I was. You've heard it: in wine there is philosophy. Pull a bum from under a railroad bridge to ask him why he's never done anything with his life but chase the grape, and he'll tell you it's better to be the head of a lizard than the tail of a dragon, or similar nonsense, nine times out of ten, for he fancies himself a sage. The wino will fool himself into thinking he's a better man than the average taxpayer and a bona-fide prince compared to a captain of industry and then justify his non-stop binge with bogus philosophy. Not one in ten thousand will tell you he drinks wine because it is the cheapest way to stay drunk, period. And that's what I believed he meant by that crack. The big ingrate was calling me in a roundabout way a wino.

"Listen here," I said. "I don't have to take any lip from the likes of you." He was standing in the middle of the room. It seemed like he filled it up. Normal-size rooms and normal-size doors weren't meant for him. He was better off outside among the trees and oleander. I was afraid he was going to sit down in a chair. No furniture I had could hold him for long. I didn't want to have to buy new furniture along with everything else I had bought today. So I said, "Look, maybe you better shove off now, okay?" I didn't have any friendly feelings toward him any more. The Ulysses Cinder Philanthropic Society had bolted its doors and pulled down its shades for the day, and maybe then some.

But he just stood there. I was beginning to resent that grinning map almost as much as my stupidity. That grin was getting to be like a portable insult following me around. Then he squatted down to be closer to my level. He reached out and touched my knee. "Ulysses," he says. "I have something to tell you about myself. I think you will find it of more than passing interest."

Vi Honeycutt came in and took off all her clothes, then took off my pajamas and spread the floor with Jell-O she had brought from the kitchen in a big stainless-steel pot and we skated around on it on all fours until the ants came in and drove us off, so we went into the swimming pool and swam the Jell-O off our feet and knees until we got tired, and then she said let's go down to the beach and we did, where we got together like man and wife or better yet like a pair of mean young dogs, and lived happily ever after just that way on the sand. The End.

Did that wake you up? Well, no such thing happened. I just wanted to get your attention again, in case it started to wander. I made it up out of my head. I said I didn't care, but I can't help thinking about you who might be reading this. If you are Vi, then I'm sorry for the above nonsense.

I moved my knee out from under his hand. My hackles were up. "Is that so?" I says. He stood up again, to impress me with his size, I think, for I was hot under the collar. But I was half scared too. When a man that big puts his hand on your knee, it makes you think about what he has in mind. The kid outside was playing a faster tune on his guitar and I didn't like it at all. It put me on edge.

"Yes, it is so," he says. He walked out to the kitchen. I sat there regretting the morning with all my heart and was still sitting there thinking what a patsy I was ten minutes later when he came back carrying the container of potato salad I had just paid a dollar for. He was spooning it out with two fingers and feeding himself that way. "I am what is known as an Efrite, Ulysses," he says, his mouth full of white mash and his fingers dripping with salad dressing.

I didn't know what he meant, but it made my heart skip. "I'm too old for any monkey business," I said.

He just kept eating. I decided that the best thing to do to discourage him was to just ignore everything he said. Maybe he'd get the point. I went over to the desk by the living-room windows and picked up a letter I had gotten a few days before from my daughter, Lorna Nettles, who lives in Minnesota. I put on my reading glasses and sat down at the desk with my back turned on the big moocher. I still have the letter from Lorna, so I am able to repeat it here just as it was.

Dear Daddy,
I hope everything is fine with you. Everything is fine with us. Perry got his promotion to Office Manager and so we couldn't be better. He is on the "road to success." Little Perry and Dee-Ann are just fine. We like Minneapolis a lot. It's so clean. At least "our" part of it is. We like it a lot better than Fresno, which Perry always hated due to the summer heat and the job and, of course, the "people." You know how Perry can be when it comes to people! He can get along with anybody up to a point, but it was a real trial for him while we were in Fresno, and of course, his Office Manager there "hated his guts." I could write a "book" about that! Well, we hope everything is fine with you. We worry about you living all alone and all. A man of your years, Daddy, ought to have companions with similar interests. Don't you think so? By the way, did you get your will "taken care of" yet? I know it's not something you want to *think* about, and *we* sure don't *like* to think about it, but it really *should* be taken *care* of. "Soon." I know it can be a bother. But I have written to Mr. Harold Button, an attorney in San Soledad, who should be getting in touch with you soon with all the "necessary info." You have to be realistic, Daddy. If things don't get taken care of, then the government will "step in" and mess everything up. I remember how you used to harp about "the government." Into this and into that. Never letting people live in "peace." Well, anyway, I thought I should mention it. We wanted to come and see you last spring but Perry had to shift his vacation time

to July and we couldn't travel in the Southwest in the middle of summer as the heat makes Perry and little Perry break out. Maybe next spring things will "work out." I know you're dying to see your grandchildren, both of whom send you "hugs and kisses."

"love,"

Lorna

I hadn't seen Lorna in seven years and had never met her husband, Perry. She sends a snapshot of the kids once a year, but I've never seen them in the flesh. There was another letter from someone wanting me to join a club for senior citizens. It was a form letter and the purple ink was blurry. It went something like this:

Dear Senior Citizen!
Maybe you never thought of it this way, but your twilight years can and ought to be the most rewarding of your entire life! As one embarks upon the sunset epoch of his/her life . . .

The last paragraph of the letter asked for money. So I read the grain of the desk top instead, hoping to hear the front door open and shut—no need for goodbyes—but it didn't.

"Ah, Ulysses," he said. It made me jump. He was standing right behind me, practically breathing down my neck. "Those are very poor letters indeed. You should receive better. Tell me now—do you know what an Efrite is?"

I had a nervous hunch that this was going to be permanent, his hanging around me. I might not be able to get rid of him at all! That's what I thought. My shaky hands rattled the letter I was holding. I'm old and a bit frail now and he was big and a lot younger and could probably just take over everything if he wanted to. He could just move in and I'd be the one looking for handouts. When my Social Security check came, or the check from my pension fund, he'd take me out to cash it with his big hand on my neck. I couldn't say boo about it to anyone. He'd tear out the phone and watch my every move. He'd lock me in the bedroom at night. He'd fill the ice-box with potato salad and that's all we'd eat day and night seven times a week. If I got mad, he'd starve me. He'd pick the TV programs. He'd decide what time was bedtime and when we'd get up. I could almost hear him saying, "That's enough wine for you, you lousy old soak. We can't afford it, the way you drink it up." *We!* Where does he get that *we* business? But there it was, that's how things were going to turn out, and what could I do about it? Nothing!

These were stormy thoughts all right and I couldn't get my bearings while I was thinking them. How was I going to get out of this mess? Then I got hopping mad. I turned around to face him. "I don't know what a damned Efrite is or what you got in mind, but you had better get your tail back on the road before I call a cop. I helped you out and now there's nothing else I can do for you. If you have any gratitude at all for what I've done, then you will just walk out that door and get yourself a job somewhere and forget you ever saw Ulysses Cinder, even though he is probably the biggest chump you will ever be privileged to lay eyes on."

"My gratitude is boundless, Ulysses," he says.

"Then, well then, if that's so, if that's the case, then—" See, he had me stuttering. He had bowed and salaamed, and it caught me off-guard, because there was something in the gesture that wasn't at all fake. There wasn't a bit of mockery in it. For it's the kind of thing you can't do with the idea of fooling somebody, if you don't mean it and if you don't know exactly how it's done. Picture a wino trying to kiss the hand of a lady. It just wouldn't work, you see?

"I swear by the sun and its brightness, by the moon when it

follows close upon it, by the sky and Him who built it, that I am indeed in your debt, Ulysses."

I didn't know what to say. I wish you could have been there to hear the way he talked, so smooth and deep, and the way he looked, like something out of a kid's book, almost the color of smoke, and eyes glittering greenish.

"Forget it," I said. "I just don't like to see a man sorry as you. Maybe you'll go back on the eighty-cent swill and wind up naked in the park again, but I figure I did what I could."

He laughed, but not nasty. "You have helped me in ways you don't understand."

I went to the door and held it open for him, but he didn't move, so I nudged him out into the hall with my elbow. "All right," I says, just to humor him along. "What is an Efrite?" I'd figured out by now that he was crazy, though it seemed a harmless sort of lunacy. A lunatic will salaam with a lot of style and fool everyone but the doctor.

"A jinn," he says. "Perhaps 'genie' is the word most familiar to you."

I thought: Well, here is a bona-fide nut. I wasn't really all that surprised. You drink that cheap stuff long enough and you can kiss your brains goodbye. "Listen, Sadass," I says, "you've got to lay off that muscatel." Every wino in the world gets that advice now and then, though it's about as useless as trying to tell the wind which way to blow and when, but if you ever get a notion in your head to help sorry people out of the hole they've dug for themselves, then you're going to find yourself in the position of dispensing good advice, because if you only feed and clothe a bum without trying to set him straight, then you're just telling him in so many words that you approve of his way of life and that there are rewards in degeneracy.

"You of course do not believe me," he says. I shrugged, inched the door shut. "But, because you have shown me genuine kindness, kindness that proceeds purely from the heart, and for this reason alone, I am prepared to grant you any wish you desire, whatever its nature." He put his hand on the door and stopped it from closing. I couldn't budge it against his weight. I got mad. "Please, Ulysses," he says. "Test me. All doubt will be removed at your command."

"No!" I hollered. "You get out of here, you damned—" And the door slammed shut like a big wind had caught it. It made my ears ring. I figured he had let it go all at once. I waited a second and then peeked out into the hall. No one was there. He was gone. And that was just fine with me. I felt better.

I went into the kitchen, took a bottle of Pinot Noir out of the cupboard, and opened it. I felt like something dark red and heavy. I filled a glass and took it to the table by the French doors. The street was empty. He'd cleared out fast. Fine. I thought about the whole affair. It was the craziest thing that had ever happened to me. Who would have thought that they would ever meet such a fruitcake? Efrite! I had a good laugh over it, now that he was out of my life. I thought of his big moony face and the phony grin and the way he salaamed, nearly touching his feet with his head, and then I laughed even harder. I raised my glass to the empty street. "Here's to you and you and you," I said, but there were only gulls out there now, gliding around looking for edible litter. Tears from all that laughing rolled down my face. What a world!

I filled up my thermos with Pinot Noir, cut a piece of cheese and wrapped it in some wax paper along with some bread, and walked down to the beach. A little fresh air was called for after all the day's nonsense. I decided to be a little more cautious in the future with my philanthropic leanings.

I found a nice private stretch of sand next to some big rocks. I thought I'd just sit and listen to the surf for a while and speculate about nothing in particular. It was a good day for it.

Warm and blue. The rocks were covered with mooching gulls who were eyeing my cheese and bread with unconcealed avarice, but I was out of the charity business for a while. The doors were closed and the blinds were pulled down tight.

After a few cups of wine and a cheese sandwich, I laid back on the warm sand with my hands behind my head. I'd brought a hat with me to keep the sun out of my eyes and I pulled the brim down past my nose. I am prepared to grant your wish, the big loony said, and the memory of those nutty words popped suddenly into my head. Well, I had to believe it was a higher sort of lunacy than most forms of mental derangement. I mean, at least he still thought of himself as someone who was important. A lot of people with mental problems get to thinking of themselves as snakes or dogs or victims of secret societies where an assassin lies in waiting behind every potted plant. At least this Sadass figured he was in a position to do something good for people, and he was sociable enough. In the old days, nuts like that used to call themselves Napoleon or Caesar. You could tell he believed it, too. That's what the sly grin was all about. The phony-baloney grin of someone who believes he's got a big surprise up his sleeve and that no one has got a snowball's chance in Phoenix, Arizona, of figuring out what it is. If I had called his bluff, maybe it would have set things straight for the poor cluck. I thought about that. I thought about what my wish would be. Easy enough. It came clear as a bell. The one single thing that had made my life only half a life lately had been the absence of Emily. Laying there on that warm sand with my face covered up with my hat, I said out loud, "Sadass, you knuckleheaded loony, I wish she was right here, Emily Noffsinger, bring her back, you big goon, full of life, the way she used to be before she got mopey, the way I remember her before she got sick and low of spirit."

I didn't know what I was getting into. Who would?

All right. Now here comes the part that will test your swallowing ability. Like I said on page 1, I don't know who is reading this, or if anyone is, but if you're still there, whoever you are, I expect you'll toss this story of mine into the nearest litter barrel and throw in with the ones who talk about my wine drinking or the state of my cerebral health. Maybe you should. I mean, you have your way of looking at things and it's been good enough for you and you're a happy man or woman, so why tamper with a good thing, even if it doesn't come close to covering every mysterious happening you may have heard of or even witnessed yourself? That's understandable. I support it all the way. The way you make sense out of the world is probably the most important thing you have going for you. If it isn't, then you're headed for trouble you never counted on. The way you make sense out of the world is the thing that pulls you through all the setbacks in life, whether it's sickness, death in the family, or financial ruin. It's your lifeboat in a sea of unpredictable fortune. Doesn't matter if it's different from what other people think. It's always a personal matter between you, yourself, and you, even if there are fifty million people who think exactly the same thing, if you follow me. So you better hang on to it and we'll say goodbye right now. Goodbye. Let's call this

THE END

and have done with it. On the other hand, I don't want you reading on if you're going to take it all as a joke, either, just to have a good laugh with your friends. That's not why I'm doing this. The hell with you and your smirkish friends. Goodbye. You must feel real good about yourself if you can laugh at a senile old man, if that's what you take me to be.

All right. If you're still with me, you're probably thinking:

He's going to talk about thunderclaps and the parting of skies and the sound of a thousand trumpets, or the air got dim and it began to rain flower petals and a grandly solemn voice from a cloud spoke to him. But you're wrong. Nothing like that happened. It was as simple as a heartbeat and soft as a woman's hand. It *was* a woman's hand. It touched my arm and ran up the length of it to my neck. I pushed the hat off my face and sat up. And there she was. Sitting on the sand next to me. Emily Noffsinger. My Emily.

"Hello, Ulysses," she said.

She wasn't the Emily of her last years of life but the Emily of thirty-five years ago, Emily Jewel Noffsinger, and she was no whispy ghost floating in the air but full of life, warm and pink with health. She was wearing a plain white dress, the pleated kind that was popular back in the early forties, and white, short-heeled shoes, the kind they used to call wedgies.

If you're still not scoffing at me, you're probably wondering how I took it. Some people will tell you:

> *Eat the grapes,*
> *Forget the vineyard*

but I can't do that. So I took it bad. I backed away from her on all fours like a crab. I felt my mind sliding away. I actually felt it sliding away, like mud down a hillside. I got dizzy. I couldn't catch my breath. I felt weak all over and could barely hold myself closed against the sudden liquefication of my interior.

She got up and brushed the sand from her skirt. She walked toward me. The wind was blowing her hair, and her skirt was whipping around her long, pretty legs. She was smiling. It was a smile I saw, now, only in my dreams or in moments of reverie. Emily had a beautiful smile. It brought you up short and made you think that whatever it was you were doing right then wasn't the most important thing God had ever dreamed up for men to do with their time. It makes sense to say that it was a smile that raised you up above the task at hand and improved your whole outlook, at least for a time. I told you earlier that I had been irritated with Emily's retiring nature and with her not being much interested in the humdrum ups and downs of the orange-growing business, but that indifference was exactly what made that smile of hers so uplifting. It was her smile and the overriding love behind it (it's true, I can say that even now) that made my own life of petty bothers tolerable. I'd figured all this out in the seven years since her death. It's sort of like figuring out that money will buy firewood after you've set fire to your bankroll to keep your hands warm, and just about as stupid. If you follow this to the last notebook, you'll see that I soon had reason to be less hard on myself and less praiseful of Emily.

She touched my hand. I guess I was making a bawling sound. I choked on her name. It wouldn't come out. "Don't cry, Ulysses," she said. But listen, I wasn't crying out of happiness or surprise, much as I'd like to have you think so. No, I was just scared, plain and simple. I believed my brains had finally gone to mush all at once and that this was the end of me and that I'd never be able to get back to my apartment and the .38 and I would wind up in the common ward of the community hospital with a tube in my foot and another in my nose and Lorna's lawyer leaning down into my face telling me to sign a paper but it's no use for I don't remember my name.

I could see that Emily, or what appeared to be Emily, was concerned about me, but I started yelling at her anyway, like she was the last person in the world I wanted to see, instead of the first.

"Go away!" I yelled. I even said, "Begone!" like some kind of witch-scared Pilgrim. And that did it. She *was* gone. Quick as a finger snap. Nothing there in front of me but a view of the beach and the resort hotel at the other end of it and the white line of breakers rolling up to its sea wall. I felt sick. Like I'd been punched down low, hard. I puked.

This ends notebook 2.

## *Here begins notebook 3.*

Kneeling down on the sand upchucking, I heard a voice above me say, "Most unfortunate."

I looked up. Up on one of the big rocks among the gulls was Sadass himself. He climbed down.

"You of course did not prepare yourself. I am not to blame. It was simply too much for you to absorb, my friend. It was a shock."

He put his hand on my shoulder. I looked at him. There was that damnable face.

I still felt sick and crazy, but I hit him on the grin anyway. As hard as I could. Then I passed out cold.

Where did the time go? I'm late for supper. I'll get back to this tomorrow. Got to eat, then I want to watch TV for a while, then to bed. I didn't think it would take this long to put all of what happened down on paper. I'm tired.

Okay. This is another day. I feel fine, even though I dreamed about dying again. Not a nightmare, though. I was made out of air and floated through the world and above it, and then I was solid again and walking barefoot on wet green leaves somewhere else. Many people I knew and didn't know said, Hello, Hello, all smiles. A tall man in a white robe stepped down from a gold golf cart and picked a flower that was growing on the fairway. He gave the flower to a woman. The woman gave it to a man. The man gave it to a child. The child gave it to me. I had a thought in the dream that everything was so simple when you saw it clearly. Of course, when I woke up, it was all nonsense. What seems clear as crystal in dreams is often garbled in real life. You have had that experience yourself, probably.

Back to my tale. I woke up in my own bed, staring up into a face I didn't want to see, but at least I wasn't in any hospital. It looked as though it was going to be tougher to get rid of him than a plague of aphids. Well, like they say:

> *What the doc can't cure,*
> *You'd best learn to endure.*

It was some comfort, though, to see that I had split his lip pretty good—hah!—an old man like me.

But he didn't seem sore about it. "My gift, it is serious, Ulysses," he says. "There are dangers."

"Suppose I say I don't want any part of you or your so-called gift?"

He shrugged and salaamed. "I hear and obey on the head and the eye," he says, and starts to fade away. I could see the wall behind him by looking straight into his big gut. But he was disappearing slow, not all at once like Emily did, who went away so quick it was like she was wired to a light switch, and even after a full minute of this he was still there in the room, or at least an outline of him was.

"Okay," I says, feeling sly. "Come back here." He got solid again and squatted next to the bed. I said: "Let's have some

Ruby Port, a quart of it, that sweet stuff that goes for five or six dollars a bottle, and let's have it just a hair under room temperature."

A fancy, red-labeled bottle popped into his hand. He uncorked it, produced a crystal goblet worth a buck in any hardware store, and poured out a working dollop. I sat up and took the glass. It was good stuff, not a cheap imitation. I stuck a finger in it and watched it form into a red drop on the tip. I tasted it. It was real. The pure quill. I felt sly as a cat.

"You ought to go on the stage," I says. I made my voice sound a little bored, like I'd seen it all.

"You think this is parlor magic?" he says. "The parlor magician practices illusion, Ulysses. I produce reality."

I was amazed right then at the smooth products of a diseased brain. "So, you're a real genie," I says, mumbling into my goblet. I knew now that I was talking to myself. The dying brain can play tunes no one ever heard. I slid out of bed. My heart was thumping not so much from the exertion of getting up as from the decision I had come to all at once under the influence of that imaginary wine.

"Indeed I am," he says, standing aside in lackey fashion as I left the room. "Although I prefer the term Efrite. I believe it has more dignity."

"Dignity? Is that so, is that so?" I says, pretending to be curious as the dickens and amiable as a shoe salesman. I felt slyer than anything that had ever lived under a rock.

I went out to the living room. I was casual about it. Like I was just trying to get my legs under me again, like I was taking a little stroll through my apartment to stretch out my leg muscles. I yawned. I scratched. I went to the bookshelf and took down the book about the flowers, fruits, and trees, and such, and palmed the key. I pretended to be hunting for something and flipped through a dozen pages or so before I put the book back into its slot. Then I got the teakwood box out and opened it.

He was standing about ten feet from me, grinning again in that smart-ass way, like he was a step or two ahead of me and always would be. So I leveled the gun at him and pulled the trigger. The noise set off a firebell in my ears. The slug hit the wall behind him and I heard a bunch of dishes fall off the shelf in the kitchen. A blind southpaw with his left arm amputated at the collarbone couldn't miss a target that size from a few yards away, but the slug didn't leave a mark on him, and a spray of rainbows flew out of the place where the bullet had gone into him and from where it came out in back, and the room glowed for a few seconds with the full spectrum, and he just stood there grinning, without a hint in his face that he'd just been gunned at close range.

Well, I figured I'd seen enough. Of him. Of everything. I didn't intend to spend the last few years of my life condemned to take the creatures of a failing brain seriously. So I put the barrel of the .38 in my mouth and squeezed down on the brass trigger. The key in the lock, I waited for the last door to open.

The gun went off. There's no doubt in my mind about that. WHAP! But I didn't fall down. I didn't feel anything. I heard the bullet slam into the mirror on the wall behind me, heard glass tinkle in a heap, heard the echo of the explosion come rifling back to me from the street though the French doors, but I was still standing on my two feet, still alive, my heart was still thudding in my ears, the electric clock in the kitchen was still humming, and him, Sadass the so-called genie, he was still standing in front of me, the last human face I'd ever have to see, except that it wasn't human. I looked at the gun. I touched the barrel. It was hot. The air smelled of gunpowder.

I decided: no one was ever this crazy. Will you go along with that?

So I must be sane. Whatever that word meant, probably the sorriest word in the dictionary, sane as I ever was at least, sound of mind, like they say, and this big goon was exactly what he said he was, a full-fledged Efrite ugly as sin, a genie straight out of Arabian Nights come to San Soledad to meddle in the life of a retired orange grower for no clear reason other than bedevilment.

"I perceived in your eyes a true reluctance, Ulysses," he says, "and I took it upon myself to interpret that reluctance as a request for invulnerability to bullets, at least for the moment. As the bone and tissue of your skull and brain parted before the destroying bullet, I made instantaneous repairs in its wake."

"Thanks," I said. I noticed that he was sweating.

"I hope I was not in error?"

I thought about it. No, I didn't want to die. Probably no suicide does. It's just that when you find yourself painted into a corner through no fault of your own, there's nothing else to do but go out the nearest window. Of course a lot of people have ways of fooling themselves into thinking they are not in a corner. Not me. I know a corner when I see it.

I shook my head. "No," I said. I found the bottle of Ruby Port and took it into the kitchen. I filled the goblet. Drank. Filled it again. Drank. Again. Then I sat down. He joined me at the table. I poured myself another glass. I didn't offer him any. A drunk giant was bad enough. A drunk genie could spell real trouble.

"So what happens next?" I says.

He showed me the palms of his hands. "Anything you desire, effendi."

"What about the tin lamp?"

"Tin lamp?"

"You're supposed to come out of a tin lamp, or maybe it's a brass lamp. When I rub it, remember? Don't you know the story?"

There was that grin again, splitting his heathen face. "Literary symbolism, Ulysses. A device to impart the impression of meaning to that which is essentially inexplicable. It suggests to the closed organization of the exclusively rational mind that the power I represent is containable and that it is at the command of he who possesses it, without regard to his moral and intellectual qualities or the intentions that derive therefrom."

It was hard to concentrate on what he was saying. It took me a while to sort out what he meant with his fancy six-bit words. "Say, do you have to talk like that?" I says. "Like you just got your doctor degree in flummydiddle from the university?"

"How would you prefer that I express myself, effendi?"

"Like a normal everyday American, that's how!" I thought if I was going to be stuck with him, then I'd better be able to figure out what he was saying to me, for you don't want to misunderstand the intentions of a genie.

The look on his face changed. "What I'm trying to tell you, Ulysses," he says, dropping his fancified tone, "is that all the crap about tin lamps and magic carpets was the work of some peckerwood jerk-offs who couldn't get hold of a hard idea if it grew handles."

"That's better," I said.

I didn't feel like talking for a while. I needed some time to digest everything that had happened, even though there wasn't enough time left in creation for that to happen. I could see he was getting fidgety while I pondered things. Too bad.

But then he just can't hold back any more and he says, "Well?"

"Well what?" I says. I knew what he meant, though.

"What happens next, Ulysses? The ball's in your court."

"Suppose you tell me."

"You still don't get it, do you? I *belong* to you, old-timer. I'm your personal genie. You can have anything you want, no holds barred. You can make whatever happens next in the world the result of your own whims. Get the idea? Listen, Ulysses, as of now you're tied in to the dynamos that keep the whole parade trotting along the boulevard. It's a gift, free of charge, no questions asked."

I'd been hearing a siren get closer and closer and finally the squad car itself turned up the street and rolled to a screeching stop at the curb in front of the apartment building. Someone must have heard those shots and called down the law on us.

Sadass looked out the windows. Just looked. No hocus-pocus, no hand-waving, no secret mumbo-jumbo words. Maybe his eyes bugged out a little, maybe his forehead grew a few more wrinkles, but I figured that was for my benefit—to sort of impress me with the idea that it took real effort on his part to pull these tricks off. Anyway, whatever the reason, the squad car and the two cops who had just been about to climb out of it disappeared. Where they had been parked, there was now a pair of jabbering birds the size of chickens. Not local birds, but some kind of fancy red, green, and blue birds with little pale beaks and big glassy yellow eyes. They pecked around in the street for a few minutes, then flew off in a ruckus of flapping and squawking, as if they'd just figured out that they weren't in the proper jungle any more.

"Wait a minute," I said. "What about those cops? They've got families to go home to. You can't just turn them into birds for our convenience."

"Believe me, they're going to be a whole lot happier as birds." He had a smug look on his face, proud, I guess, of what he had done, but there were beads of sweat on his lip and he looked pained.

"That's not the point," I says. "You can't just turn a man into a bird and feel like you've done him a favor."

He looked at me as if I'd said something in Greek. "Why not?" he asks. He actually looked puzzled.

"Why not? I'll tell you why not. Because you *can't*. That's why not. Now undo what you did, we'll have to figure another way to deal with them."

He looked out the window at the sky. I followed his gaze. Two shapes were dropping like stones. It was the cops. They stopped falling when they were about fifty feet from the pavement. They came the rest of the way down slow and easy and landed on their feet. But something was wrong with them. They were looking down at their feet. They didn't have any feet. What they had sticking out of the ends of their uniforms were bird claws. Big gray crusty-looking bird claws. The cops started howling. One had taken out his gun and was pointing it at his new feet. The other cop was throwing up his lunch. It was a sorry sight.

"Son of a bitch," says Sadass, wiping his damp forehead with the back of his arm. "I heard that things like this could happen, but I never believed it. Look at those poor bastards. This doesn't sit well with me, Ulysses."

"It doesn't sit well with *you*? How the hell do you think *they* feel about it?" We were yelling at each other and I'm sure the cops could have heard us if they weren't already preoccupied with their own problems.

"Dammit all to hell!" says my big genie, slapping his forehead with the butt of his hand, making sweat fly. "Ulysses, these are very strange times!"

"Tell me something I don't know," I says, hoisting my glass.

He leaned out the French doors and looked down at the messed-up cops with a fierce gaze, giving it all he's got. The sweat started dripping off his chin. His eyes were more out than in. I felt a little giddy. Wine, I guess. Plus the events of the day. I began to sing a little ditty we used to sing in grammar school:

> I wouldn't marry a schoolteacher,
> I'll tell you the reason why,
> She blows her nose in yellow corn bread
> And calls it punkin' pie.

I noticed in an absent-minded sort of way that Sadass was cutting huge farts, like a horse will under a heavy load sometimes.

> Jesus, lover of my soul,
> Lead me to the sugar bowl.

His neck was bulging and the veins were standing out from the skin like they wanted to be free.

> Betty baked an apple cake
> In a rusty pan.
> People will be mean
> Whenever they can.

He was holding his breath now and grunting. Just like a pig. He was also shaking. But, one foot at a time, the cops got their proper feet back. It took a while and they were in poor mental shape by the time it was over with. They were sitting on the curb. They had their arms around each other and were rocking back and forth, bawling their heads off. They were blubbering like tots left alone by their mama.

> If a body meet a body in a bag of beans,
> Can a body tell a body what a body means?

"I didn't figure on it being like this," says Sadass, ignoring my little rhymes. "I mean, if I'd known about it, I wouldn't have turned them into birds so fast without including a safety hatch. I'll tell you something, old-timer: it was a fight to reverse that stunt."

"Figured what would be like what?" I says, but without any real confidence that he was going to clear anything up for me.

"A mathematician, a vizier by the name of Ibn Al-Haitham, once explained it to me in Bassorah. No one took him seriously back in those days when miraculous happenings were more or less commonplace. But he was way ahead of his time. I myself figured that he had just misjudged the situation. But it looks to me like that old number juggler was right."

"I don't have any idea of what you're talking about," I says, pouring out another glass of that wine, which is about the best Ruby Port I have ever tasted.

"That old boy talked about how the future was going to be different. It was going to be rough, according to him. He said the world—but by that he meant what you call the Universe—is sort of like a top slowing down more and more and starting to wobble. He didn't mean it *looked* like a top, but only that it acted like one. He said that in the future it was going to start loosening up around its center, like a rotten peach around its stone. Sorry to have to tell you this, effendi."

"I'll try to live with it," I says, and he gives me a funny look, like I'd hurt his feelings or something.

"It's no joke. When that wobbling starts, all sorts of tricky shit starts hitting the fan. Things get undependable. Like what happened to those cops. You people even have a name for it. I read it in one of your magazines. *Entropy.*"

"Never heard of it."

The cops out in the street were beginning to attract a lot of attention. They were standing together on the sidewalk, looking, now, like a pair of manikins, white and stiff. Then one of them sat down suddenly and took off his boot. He held his foot in both hands and rocked back and forth like a child with its favorite stuffed toy. The other cop knelt down and began to count his partner's toes.

Then the spectators scattered. Something else was coming down out of the sky. It was the squad car. It didn't slow up before it hit. I guess Sadass forgot about it or was too bushed to put on the brakes. It smashed into the street and bounced up and toppled into a parked van. A bunch of hubcaps rolled away from the wreckage. This was the last straw as far as those two cops were concerned. They had seen enough. They got up and sprinted away from this terrible place. I saw that one of them still had a pair of blue wings poking out of his shirt collar. The wings were pretty useless, but they were flapping anyway, as if they could lift the two-hundred-pound constable to safety.

"I don't know anything about any rotten peaches," I says. "But you better do something for those cops down there, and do it quick."

He took to pacing around the room. "Well," he says. "There are two ways of going about it. Two angles of attack. There's *time*—that's one angle. And there's *space*—that's the other angle. Now *space*, there's your pure son of a bitch, according to old Ibn Al-Haitham."

I saw the cops disappear around the corner at the east end of the block. A few people were following behind, hoping that the side show wasn't over. Some kids were poking around the wrecked squad car and van. Another siren was coming closer and closer. The street was filling up like it was Fat Tuesday in New Orleans.

"Time might be the easier way to go. See, when you're dealing with spatial transformations of physical entities, you're in a one-on-one situation—you against the local laws of physics. The results are pretty spectacular, but it takes a whole lot of energy. This entropy business seems to have played hell with the process, which used to be a snap. So let's work with time. Just for the fun of it. What do you say?"

"You're the Efrite," I says.

"Right, little buddy," he says. "That I purely am. So here goes nothing." He poked a finger at the kitchen clock. "Watch the hands. When it winds backward twenty minutes, give a holler." He shut his eyes, gritted his teeth, and cut another eye-burning fart. It took him about a minute to restart the world twenty minutes back. The cops, who had been birds a little later but who wouldn't be again if everything went right, pulled up to the curb and got out of the squad car, which didn't have a dent on it or a hubcap missing. Sadass groaned. He grabbed the kitchen clock and growled at it, and the cops backed up into the car the way they came and the car screeched off in reverse, picking up speed backwards until it disappeared. The busted mirror had snapped back together and jumped up on the wall. It was like a movie in reverse. The bullet holes had disappeared and the faint smell of gunpowder was replaced by the smell of shaving lotion or maybe air freshener.

"Everything outside our skulls just backed up twenty-two minutes. Catch that sweet smell? That's the odor of time. Pretty nice, right?" He looked like a cat with feathers in its mouth. I decided that I would stay drunk as long as I could stand it.

Vi, you aren't reading this, not this far at least, but if you are, I just want to tell you how much I appreciated that last massage. I feel like a new man today.

What happened was, she came in holding a bottle of medicine in her hand. "I never saw that before," I said, like a damn fool, for she hadn't accused me of anything yet.

"Oh, haven't you," she said.

"Honest, Vi. I never used that stuff in my life."

"Hardy-har-har, Mr. Cinder. I am *laugh*ing." But she wasn't really sore about it. She likes to buffalo a man, and the way she does it, no one really minds. Besides, she is such a good-looker you wouldn't care if she *was* mad, just to have her around a little longer.

"I don't even know what is in that bottle," I said.

"Fibber! You know exactly what is in this bottle!"

She held it in my face. Kaopectate.

"You've been plugging yourself up on purpose just so you'd get a freebie peristaltic massage out of me, now don't you lie!"

I'd left the damn bottle in the bathroom along with my shaving kit. But I put my glasses on and squinted at the bottle like I'd never seen it before. I moved my lips as if the word Kaopectate was strange to me.

But Vi just laughed and whipped off my covers and began to give me the massage of my life. It damn near hurt. But when she was through, I had to get up and trot to the bathroom, for she got things so loosened up I damn near messed my pajamas.

Well, a little later, Sadass and I were taking a stroll. We went toward downtown, to take in the sights, Sadass being a stranger to the area.

What follows is a little hard for me to remember right. I have gone over it a few times in my mind, but I might have some parts of it mixed up, or misspelled. But you will get a general idea of what it's all about. On the little stroll into town, Sadass decided to tell me the story of how he came to be lying naked in the park ten thousand miles from his usual haunts.

Here's more or less what he said:

"A little French egghead who called himself Antoine Galland is the fella that did me in, Ulysses." (We were downtown by this time, down on the waterfront watching tuna boats unload.) "He was a shrewd little bugger. He made a trip to Constantinople back in the year 1691 along with a bunch of diplomats. Well, this Galland—who was a college professor, not a diplomat—got to snooping around some old manuscripts in the big library there, and sure enough, he stumbles on this old formula. Now this smart little frog is not your average browser but a top-flight scholar. In fact, he is Europe's number-one expert in Oriental languages and history. But even at that, he didn't know garbage from tossed salad about old Araby and the real mysteries that originated there. It was this formula he ran across that opened the gate for him. Now this formula comes from Egypt and is just about as old as handwriting itself. It's probably one of the very first things people figured out about the world. The Magi—the Egyptian experts in science and magic—were the ones responsible for keeping it safe and out of the hands of yokels, asswipes, and lunatics. See, there are general and changeless laws of wisdom. Most religions are built on them, but they get to be so mucked over by the boobs that no one can figure out what they mean after a time. I'll give you a for-instance: nobody today knows what an angel is. You probably got some kind of horsed-up notion that they are big bird-men with blond hair, good teeth, and kindly dispositions, but watch out! An angel is pure mind acting in a narrowly allotted perimeter of thought so as to concentrate its power. But I won't say any more about that. That's another can of worms. I'll just give you this bit of advice: Keep on your toes. Everything goes downhill from Egypt, my friend. Those were the days! You think the Greeks were smart? Shit-fire! Everything they knew came from Egypt. Plato himself went there to become a Magus but he couldn't hack it. Angel of morning, angel of night, angel of solitude, angel of despair, angel of the instincts, angel of death, angel of music, on and on and on. I see from your newspapers that you people are space travelers. But your knowledge is the toymaker's knowledge. Your head is a bit fat. Nothing personal, now. Mind, reason, and will. You use them to make toys. It's kind of like using elephants to crack walnuts. You get Jumbo to crack the nut, then wonder how in the world you are going to move that load of timber from the depot to the mill, never once thinking that that big pretty-eyed monster with the telephone-pole legs might just do the trick. It's exactly the same thing. Anyway, this Antoine Galland is not dumb in that way, although the world by his time is pretty much on the road toward backwards-thinking. So there he is in the library at Constantinople going over the old manuscripts when he comes across the formula the old Magi had kept for all those centuries down underneath the pyramids and in other safe places. Are you getting all this? Is it clear? Look, I personally am no angel. But I'm not a devil either, like some people hold. Look at it this way: I am an instrument. And like your typical instrument, I can be put to good use or bad, depending on the user. Of course, certain safeguards are built into the process. I'll get to that later. Here's something you may not know: Constantinople was dedicated to the Virgin Mary on May 11, 330. Constantine, the emperor of Rome, killed his wife, his son, his wife's brother, his wife's brother's little boy, his wife's brother's little boy's little dog, suffering an attack of conscience as a result. Now there was this philosopher and dabbler into the occult sciences named Sopater who told

Constantine that the only way to make sure his bad con-science didn't up and do him in was to get rid of pagan polytheism and the arcane practices that went along with it. Otherwise, he would find himself ten miles up shit's creek without an oar. See, the emperor had nothing to look forward to each night but bad dreams and bloody ghosts. Constantine surrounded himself with Christian bishops then, and they told him that God would forgive his murdering ways if he would only get rid of those magic-practicing reactionaries and establish Christianity as the number-one state religion. They told him that the old pagan temples were secret meet-ing places where the die-hard reactionaries were plotting against him. Well, Constantine turned Christian then and there and came down hard on the old pagans. He wiped them out. This is how come you are a Christian today. That's how it all began, on the official level, I mean. Anyway, some of the pagans managed to escape the Christian storm troopers. They went underground and took the old knowledge with them. Of course, the whole melee was a result of a major misunder-standing to begin with, plus a lot of wholesale paranoia, which in those unsophisticated days was limited to ass-crimping terror without any fancy twists. See, the old pagans also believed in only one God, but they went on to say that there was a passel of minor gods, who were personifications of His various and sundry attributes—how else, they said, can you get a clear picture of God unless you can arrange to see all His scattered qualities, some of which are in direct con-tradiction of others? The white-bearded grandfather with lightning snapping out of his fingernails wasn't good enough of a picture for them. They saw the whole universe as a huge painting where God Himself was Painter and Painting both. But nobody at the time wanted to sit down over a glass of muscatel and reason it out. No, they wanted to kick ass, take names, and spoon-feed the rabble. And that's the way it's been, I take it, ever since." He looked at me, but I just shrugged, not knowing much about such things. "Anyway, getting back to our man in Constantinople—Antoine Galland, the frog scholar—it was him who dug up the old formula that had been hidden away by the pagans who Constantine persecuted. Now, there are formulas and there are formulas. I understand that the formula for the atomic bomb takes up only about a page or less. The one Antoine Galland found took up a one-thousand-page book! He found it under a loose floorboard in an unused wing of the library—he bribed a guard to let him in—and it was all done in handwriting, and it was in Greek! Hell's bells, it took that little Frenchie a year just to read the thing through enough times so that he was sure he understood all the fine points. The last thing he had to do was travel to Egypt. There's a big stone critter there called the Sphinx. You've probably heard of it. It's got the head of a woman, the body of a bull, the feet of a lion, and is equipped with the wings of an angel. Some people thought those wings were eagle's wings, but they aren't. They are the wings of a materialized angel. This big edifice is also a building. Inside, it is honeycombed with secret passageways and rooms and what-all. In a big square room down deep inside, the final details of the formula were to be carried out. Galland had to spend a week there in the spooky dark, without food, and only one cup of water a day, saying special prayers, as the formula instructed. After that, he made seven circles all with the same center, using strips of metal. Lead, tin, iron, copper, mercury, silver, and gold. He had to cover these circles with a small pyramid of cypress poles. Then he had to drape a sheet that had come from the bed of a woman who had died giving birth to a three-eyed freak over this pyramid. Then a cup of ram's blood sprinkled all around the contraption. Then more praying. It went on like this—water, fire, long-dead languages written in blood, innards of strange animals, the tongues of birds, disgusting mess, actually—but the end result of all this was *me*. I broke out of a warm volcanic baby moon, an asteroid I guess you'd call it, which is stationary in space, directly over Damascus, where I'd been resting peacefully for quite a few centuries thanks to a Magus who knew what he was doing, and I fell into the world, air streaming around me, the sounds and smells of the old planet filling my head, and the next thing you know I'm kowtowing in front of the Frenchie, saying, 'I hear and obey on the head and the eye,' just like the old days. The first thing he wants is something to eat and a bottle of wine, because of all the deprivation he'd undergone just to get hold of a genie. He was a smart cookie and so he held off making any big requests until he had restored himself to his normal way of life. He wanted to go back to France to collect his wits, sort out his thoughts, and figure out exactly why he had summoned me in the first place. He knew he had to be damn careful about his motives. He knew there was a big danger in going overboard. It took him a month of pondering before he made up his mind about what he wanted me to do for him. He wanted knowledge. He wanted to know every last thing there was to know about old Araby, from culinary habits to religious celebrations, and I gave it to him. And that was it. That's all he wanted. I told him that there was a lot more to the world than specialized scholarship—power, fame, money, women, love—just to name a few, but he only shook his head and said, 'Nope, those are the usual mundane temptations, and they lead to boredom at best and black despair at worst. It's knowledge I require, Efrite, and it's knowledge that you are going to give me.' I'll say this, the little frog knew his own mind. After I gave the bookworm what he wanted, he gave another week's thought to what he wanted to do with me then. He decided to send me to the other side of the world—the formula didn't tell him how to get me back into the asteroid—and I wound up in the park you found me in. I was supposed to lie there, naked and not more than half conscious, right out in the weather, until someone with *genuinely good intentions* found me. See, this Antoine was a careful man, and he had a conscience to boot, being a good Catholic. He didn't want someone with poor inclinations to come along and put me to evil use. He knew the world was stuck with me, and he did his best to neutralize any bad effects I might have on it. So off to the wilds of the New World I went, to wait for the first human with good intentions to come along. Antoine figured that would be never, being something of a cynic. Then you came along, chief. I guess I was a little groggy when you found me, and still pissed off some at Galland."

I listened to him while watching nets full of yellowtail tuna getting weighed. It was interesting, I guess, but I didn't much care how he got here. The thing was, he was *here*, he was *mine*, and now it was up to me to figure out what to do with the lummox. I guess that Frenchman, who believed he was putting Sadass out of harm's way for good, didn't count on the westward march of civilization. One of the local Indians might have found him, but being a prudent people, they probably would have left him alone.

We stood on the pier for a while just watching the boats unload. There was a nice crisp wind snapping in off the bay. I was thinking: If I had a wish coming to me—and it looked like I did—I would have this place last forever, just like it is, the dark ocean, the hard blue sky, the gulls, the long white boats, the men in their rubber boots guiding the netloads of silvery fish down to the wet dock, the slap of the water against the pilings, just let it go on and on forever, so that you could always count on it being here the way it is now, whether I myself was here or not, and nothing ever out of place. Then I *would* add Emily and myself. And then maybe get rid of nine-tenths of everybody else. But the memory of her appearance on the beach brought the hair up on the back of my neck and I put the whole idea out of my softening head.

I am coming down to the end of this notebook and it's time for lunch, so I guess I'll break it off here.

I'll use the rest of this space to doodle a little poem for you:

> *There was an old man*
> *Who had nowhere to go*
> *But through a black door*
> *That was colder than snow.*
>
> *He knocked on it once,*
> *Then knocked again,*
> *And the voice that answered*
> *Said, Come right on in!*
>
> *But his feet wouldn't move,*
> *And his hands felt like clay,*
> *So he stayed outside*
> *For one more day.*

I like them when they rhyme.

*Number 4.* These are short little things when you think that they cost seventy-nine cents apiece. If I'd known how long this was going to be, I would have used something else, like one of those big tablets grade-school kids use.

Too late now.

But when you consider that a wino can buy a fifth of fortified Tokay for the same price, it begins to make you wonder about the relative worth of things and the way prices are set.

I don't believe for a minute that prices are based on a thing's actual worth.

It's all monkey business. I could tell you a thing or two about that. Like how the big canning companies put the screws to the growers. It almost made me sick when I first went into the business. But then I learned to live with it, like most farmers do.

Sometimes you'll see a farmer on TV and say to yourself, "What's he so sore about?" for they are nearly always sore at something. And they have got a right to be. But the average citizen can't figure out why. Well, buy a farm or an orchard. You'll get the message damned quick. If you're not stupid.

Anyway, we were standing there on the docks. Sadass had finished telling me all about how he got to San Soledad, but it still didn't make a whole lot of sense to me. I mean, beyond the fact that it sounded crazy all by itself. I mean, inside that crazy story there were things that got past me. Maybe I didn't listen close enough.

"Anything your heart desires, Ulysses," he says. "You just name it, old-timer, and you have got it. No questions asked. I'm kind of itchy to get back into action, before this entropy screws everything up even more than it already is."

I thought about it. I guess a lot of men would have jumped at this opportunity like a dog on a pork chop. A lot of men would start out by getting themselves a nice new car, some nice clothes, a wallet stuffed with money, and maybe a nice house in some fancy neighborhood. Then they would get grander ideas and put themselves inside a castle and surround themselves with butlers and maids. An old man would make himself young again, a worthless man would make himself president or king, a greedy man would become sole owner of everything he laid his eyes on, a dumb man would make himself smart as Einstein, not knowing that his new brains would let him figure out things that might make him miserable and depressed. They would drive themselves crazy in short order, because one dumb wish would lead to another, and the dissatisfaction in the pit of their hearts would just get bigger and bigger with each new wish, like the appetite of a dog with a growing tapeworm. Oh, they would stay content for a while, until the thrill wore off at least, but the gnaw of that empty place deep inside would start in again, and before you know it, they'd be wishing to be the Creator Himself on the golden throne juggling stars and planets and sending gangs of angels flapping through space to carry out official policy or to scare the living piss out of rebels. It just isn't right. I don't believe that Antoine Galland was happy at all after his new heap of information about the Arabs made him the top dog of all time among the professors of such things. Men, considering what they are, had better stay puny and backward if they know what's good for them or if they have any foresight at all. You may not agree with that opinion, but just take a long look at your newspaper tomorrow morning and think again.

So I says, "I had a good life. My memories are still good. I miss my Emily. I don't know whether or not I'll ever get to see her again, but if it isn't in the cards, then I don't want to be the one to tamper with the way things are supposed to be." It was partly a lie, though, because I did have weak moments, like when I tried to use Dad's .38 on myself—for surely suicide is a way of interrupting the proper order of things, and I had made a vow to myself to carry out such an interruption—but generally speaking, I believed that the use of magic to tamper with things and the way they are supposed to turn out wasn't right.

"Commendable," he says, with a trace of contempt in that big heathen face of his.

"You think so? I think it's just common sense."

"Damned uncommon, as a matter of fact."

We walked along the waterfront without talking. I think he was a little sore at me. Well, that was *his* problem, not mine. I sure as hell never rubbed his tin lamp.

We passed a seafood restaurant and stopped to look into the smoky windows. There were a lot of people inside hogging down filets, shellfish, and fries. They were smoking and drinking and talking and laughing.

"Look at that," says Sadass, acting all pissed off. "Not a goddamned thing ever changes, does it?"

"What do you mean?" I says.

"I mean all those people in there. Haven't got the first flicker of an *idea* about the pickle they are in as human beings. It's always the same, unconscious bunch of boobs yelling and laughing like time isn't going to run out on them. Shit, only the garnishings change—and for the worse, the way I see it."

I got hot under the collar. "What would you know about it? Locked up on a moon, then stuck naked under a shrub for three hundred years! How does that qualify you to pass on the way these people carry out their lives? Besides, what are they supposed to do, sit in their apartments and bawl their heads off or suck martinis down just because nothing is going to work out in the long run?"

But he ignores me, sort of, and says, "They just don't have the first flicker, do they?"

"Don't they? Where do you get off making them out to be boobs? They're people. People, a lot of them anyway, know the deck is stacked against them, and the ones that don't, they find out sooner or later, regardless. A college degree isn't required for that. You're the kind of sourball know-it-all that sees a crowd of people having a good old time and figures you are witnessing Idiots-in-Action, the Southern California chapter. You talk like one of those constipated professors who goes to a party as the honorary wet blanket, then, after swilling down half the punch, goes home to write an article about how dumb most people are, hinting all the while what a smart son of a bitch *he* is. Didn't it ever occur to you that it's better to dance than to crawl on your belly when the outcome is going to be the same, no matter what you do? If there is a God in the sky, and I personally believe there is, then it stands to reason that He figured out how things would turn out a long time ago and no fancy antics on your part are going to change His mind about it."

He gave me a pained look, like I had hit home, but only in a half-baked way. "It's an old shopworn argument, Ulysses, if there ever was one. It's been ripped apart with regularity by smarter men than you in the past ten thousand years."

I looked him in his glittering eye. "Is that so?" I says, glittering a bit in the eye too, for I figured I had him in a trap. "Well, if that's the case, if it's *needed* to be ripped apart that many times for ten thousand years, then it must be a pretty crusty notion with a lot of life to it."

He just looked at me and shook his head slowly, as if *I* was the dumb one who couldn't add or subtract, much less entertain a simple idea. I felt like hitting him again. But I didn't. Instead, I turned and walked into the restaurant, which was called Enrico's. I felt like having a glass of white wine, and my legs were a little tired.

The woman in the classy black dress who seated people took a long look at us. She tried to hold her friendly smile in place, but then started to fidget around nervously. "Table for two," I says, ignoring her problems.

"Two?" she says, like the number 2 is a little out of reach for her undersized brain. Sadass in his Goodwill clothes doesn't inspire public confidence. But she finally gets a grip on herself and shows us to a table in a dim corner, far from the main group of eaters. It's fine with me. I just want a glass of Sauterne and maybe another one after that, and a place to rest my legs.

It's a nice place, Enrico's. I often come here just to sit in a corner and watch all the people. They always have themselves a good time, most of them being tourists. Well, why shouldn't they? This is life and how it's lived. I will sometimes go over to the airport terminal with the same notion in mind. To watch travelers. Of course, travelers have more on their minds and aren't usually in a festive mood. Even so, I enjoy the all-business way they move through the waiting rooms with their luggage or how they come off a plane with a look of relief on their faces. Deep down inside, no one really believes those big howling crates have any right to fly, but they can't cancel the evidence of their own eyes, so off they go once again into the wild blue yonder, but when they get back down to earth and the dependable feel of the ground under their feet, they are always secretly grateful to be alive and it shows on their faces as a kind of a surprised excitement. I go to a lot of places in the spirit of curiosity: bus depots, the railroad station, the movies, baseball games, for there is always something new to learn about what people do, how they do it, and why. I even go to funerals—but only if I am well fortified with wine, because what you see in the faces of mourners is sometimes contagious, whether you know them personally or not.

I noticed that Sadass was looking the crowd over, too. Just sort of enjoying himself with his big feet stuck out almost all the way to the next table, which is luckily unoccupied. There was a three-piece Mexican band playing and singing over on a small stage by the bar. The song they were playing was a sad one about love lost for good, the kind the Mexicans specialize in, and I felt my eyes misting over and stinging, as if the Mexicans were cutting onions instead of strumming guitars. Those Mexicans know about the other side of love, and they build it into their music.

"You know," I says. "It sure would be nice to have Emily here with us. This is the kind of place she liked so much. She could sit and sip a glass of Port and listen to those gloomy love songs played like that and be happy as a bird. You'd never get her out camping in a tent, or out on a fishing boat, but a place like this would make her day."

Sadass gives me a funny look. Then I remembered. "Wait a

minute," I says. "Don't you pull anything. I didn't say I wanted you to make her show up in a white dress."

"But if you have one true longing in your heart, then it's for your wife. Correct me if I'm wrong."

"Okay. You're right. Does that make you feel smart? Of course, she is the one person in this world I miss. The one-trillionth part of the world that was her was a full nine-tenths of mine, but you probably don't understand that kind of arithmetic."

"Then—"

"Then nothing. No tampering. I already told you how I felt about that."

"But there is another way, Ulysses. If you've got the belly for it."

I squinted at him. A little bird in my ear was telling me to watch out. "What other way?" I says.

"*You* can go see *her*, instead of *her* coming to see *you*. It's a tough trip, but I think it can be done. What I need to do is eat a whole lot, because of the rate I'm using up energy."

"She's dead," I says.

Sadass tinged his fork against my glass. A little-bell sort of sound. His face was lit up in a Mexican-bandit type of smile, as if something struck him very comical, such as my stupidity. "That's right," he says. "She is dead."

"I don't want to discuss it," I says. I got up. "Come on. Let's go. This Mexican misery music is getting on my nerves."

We walked uptown, on Broadway, past all the clip joints where young sailors and marines loitered waiting for something good to happen to them, past the porno movie houses and the scabby winos waiting to get in so they could sip and sleep and hope that something on the screen would remind them that they were alive, the narrow jewelry stores with the small display windows showing pinhead diamonds in rings priced ten times more than they were worth, the so-called penny arcades where every pastime cost two bits or more, the walk-up nameless hotels where illegal aliens waited for their phony Social Security cards and driver's licenses to be printed up.

We walked until things started to look better: travel agencies, clean cafés, bars with padded doors studded with brass rivets, movies with decent, family marquees, taco stands, sandwich shops, health-food stores, groups of ordinary citizens shopping with money in their wallets and purses and without a devious thought clouding their faces, and then we finally reached Pizarro Plaza, a small grassy place in the middle of downtown with benches and palm trees, where a Bible-hammering evangelist was harassing passers-by with threats of hell-fire, and a bunch of shaved-head yahoos wearing orange sheets were slapping tambourines and chanting some mumbo jumbo that no one, including themselves probably, understood. We watched them for a while, then went into a Greek place.

It was called the Happy Minotaur, whatever that is, and advertised 'King Size Belly Dancers Straight From Asia Minor —No Cover Charge.' It was a smoky place without much light, but after our eyes got used to the dark, we found a table near the runway, where a fat girl with a button of cut glass stuck in her belly was heaving her weight around in time to some fast Greek music played by two little oily-haired characters who looked half bored to death. Sadass picked up a menu and studied it. When the waiter came, who was also a sawed-off oily man with a sleepy look on his face, Sadass said, "Bring the roast leg of lamb with orzo, and artichokes with dill sauce. Make it a double order." The waiter didn't think this was unusual at all, at least he didn't act as if it was. I said, "Just bring me a glass of the house wine, Charlie."

By the time Sadass's pile of food came, I'd gone through about four glasses of a heavy red wine that made my ears ring. Sadass cut a piece of meat as big as a baseball and stuffed it into his mouth. As he chewed, the corners of his mouth turned down in disgust and his black nostrils widened. It was as if someone had dropped a fresh turd on his plate. Finally he swallowed it. "San Soledad ain't Athens, old-timer," he says, washing it down with hot black coffee. But it wasn't too awful, for he managed to hog down his food—which had covered more than half the table—in about five minutes flat. Then he wiped his face and neck with his napkin and went to the john.

That reminded me that I had to go, too. All the day's wine was getting to my kidneys. The belly dancer was right above our table, and though the call of nature was nearly over-powering, I sort of hated to leave in the middle of the fastest part of her routine. She was fat, no two ways about it, and not the kind of woman you'd normally think of as good-looking or would want to take out to the movies, but there was something to the way she gyrated around up there—almost as if she didn't have any bones in her body—that kept me at the table with my legs crossed against the tide. I felt a little embarrassed and amazed at myself, for I hadn't had such thoughts as these in recent memory. I was leaning back looking straight up into her rolling belly, nearly hypnotized by the glittering false stone in the middle of it and the meal-sack breasts slogging around a little higher up, which were barely held in by a silky halter that wouldn't have covered mosquito bites properly. The sight made me somewhat dizzy. Then she turned around and gave me a first-class view of her jumping rump. Now that was a thing to behold! Son of a bitch, but I had never seen anything like it! She rolled it, she made it vibrate, she let it hover like a hot-air balloon, moving it so slow that it seemed dead-stopped in the air, but it was still musical, only you had to pay close attention to see the beat. You kind of had the feeling that the music had entered her skin and was making it dimple and twitch. Then, when she finally moved off to give some other old fool a treat, I got up and went to the john, or started to, at least. But Sadass, who had just returned, stopped me.

"Don't go back in there just yet, pardner," he whispers, all mysterious.

"What's that supposed to mean?" I says. "I've got to take a leak. If I don't take it in there, then I'm going to have to take it in here."

"Listen, Ulysses, there's a couple of rough customers back in there. You don't want to tangle with them."

"Let go of my arm, goddammit! I got to take a piss! I don't care if Baby Face Nelson is in there!"

He let me go, and I left the table with a little too much speed, for I almost fell down. I was dizzy with the strong wine and the dancing of the fat girl and the smoky air. But I righted myself and aimed toward the men's room.

I didn't see anyone in there at first. But I didn't look for anyone either. I just headed for the first urinal I saw and unzipped. Then, as relief came, I heard the troublemakers scuffling around. It was an L-shaped john, the short leg of the L going around behind the row of stalls, and so you wouldn't have noticed them on coming in. I should have just walked out, but the noise didn't sound dangerous and my curiosity was aroused. I zipped up and took a peek behind the stalls.

Well, it was plain obscene! Here were two women naked as shelled clams wrestling on the floor. It was probably an argument over some turkey-necked boyfriend with tattoos of scorpions on his skinny arms—that's what I believed on seeing them—and it had gotten physical and they came into the john to settle it, only they came into the wrong one, which was easy to do, since the word "men" on the door was written in fancified Greek-looking letters, sort of like little pieces of lightning bolts, and if you were boiling mad and not too careful, you could easily wind up going through the wrong door. Now, what happened to their clothes was another matter.

Vi said, It's time for exercise, you constipated old fool. She doesn't mean it to sound disrespectful, but she is just dumb enough to say it with a little too much meaning, if you know what I mean. I don't mind. Off I go. I guess I'll use one of those three-wheeled bikes and go down to the end of the driveway and back. I don't believe in exercise. But it's a rule. Well, you've got to have rules. That's the trouble with nine-tenths of the world now. No rules. I said I was a democrat, so don't get me wrong. Even a democrat has got to live by a set of rules. Only a damned fool would doubt that. That's democrat with a small *d*. I voted Republican most of my life until the party got taken over by the big-time slickers, starting with that gigolo-looking Dewey. I voted for Truman in 1948 because he *looked* like a Republican was supposed to look. Dewey didn't look like anything. Except a gigolo.

I'm back again. I goddamned near died coming back up the hill. Vi said, "You're white as an egg!"

I gave her a thanks-very-much look, which didn't register. But she helped me to my room and undressed me and got me into the shower and waited until I finished, thinking that I might go down the drain like so much dust, but I didn't, I'm back, and here's what happened next in the Happy Minotaur.

Well, the mistake was mine. I saw it after a minute or two of gawking. It wasn't a fight at all. The grappling wasn't meant to inflict damage. It was meant for just the opposite. I felt myself get red with the embarrassment of it. But did I leave? No. I don't know what got into me. But I couldn't bring myself to do an about-face and march out. My damn feet were glued to the floor. My mouth got dry. I never was a prude, make no mistake, but I was never one to entertain degenerate notions either. I believe people ought to lead clean lives when they can. The normal goings on between man and wife should give everyone plenty of room to satisfy their fanciest ambitions. I never did approve of the way sex had become a big industry in this country and most of the rest of the world. It isn't an industry. It's private. You've got to keep the doors closed. It only makes sense. We are not dogs and cats. But the industrialists took it over, for there was money to be made. I'm not against moneymaking either, but what you do for what you get ought to be a matter of conscience. The industrialists went too far. They had taken the sweet decency of a man and a woman and put it on film for the winos to watch. In my opinion, these industrialists ought to be deported. Send them to the North Pole and let them take pictures of seals. Let the winos watch seals.

This is how I felt and how I still feel.

But like they say: The strongest oaths are straw to the fire in the blood.

It is sadly true. It is the main problem of human beings. Say one thing, do another. Seems that our most outstanding feature is hypocrisy.

What I am saying is this: I could not make myself walk out of that lavatory. I couldn't make myself stop watching those women go at it. They were big women. I figured they were queer belly dancers who had lost control of themselves. One was a blonde who must have stood six feet tall, and the other was a shorter black-haired woman. It looked like they had oiled themselves up for the occasion. I couldn't figure out why they were going at it in the men's room instead of at home or at least out in a car. They were breathing like tired horses and making low animal noises in their throats. They didn't seem to mind me standing there gawking, if they noticed me at all. But then, they didn't seem to be the self-conscious type.

Damn it to hell, what a tangle! Arms and legs sliding together like fat white snakes, kissing and licking, fingers poking and pinching, mouths yawning wide, the big tongues red and fat and quick as butterflies, the jumbo breasts slogging around, the brown nipples sticking out like corks, the wild rolling eyes! Son of a bitch but I am not going to lie to you: I felt a stirring I hadn't felt in quite a long time! It flat got to me! It made my heart unruly. My chest felt like it was going to tear itself apart. Listen, I was swollen up like a teenager and I *itched*!

I knew that I should have gotten out of there and away from those greasy women at all costs, even if I had to crawl out on my hands and knees, but still I didn't budge. It was beginning to seem like I had gotten into something that I'd have to see through to the end. This is what occurred to me. It made me feel strange. Like you couldn't, all at once, count on anything. That probably doesn't make sense. I mean, I felt like I couldn't count on myself, on what I knew about myself, on what I was supposed to be as a civilized man. It was like the whole question of what a man was supposed to be had suddenly become brand-new again and unsettled. You think that what you do always comes from some common-sense decision, but it all at once didn't seem that way to me at all. What you do is part of a larger plan that you'll never get to see or figure out. That's how I felt. It's an awful notion. I hated it. But it was also a stimulating notion. I'll tell you, I felt stimulated! I felt hot to trot! A man of more than seventy years!

Watching those hefty queer dancers, I thought: What a dummy I am! Here I had a genuine Efrite working for me and I hadn't even used him to get what every old man on the face of this miserable old planet wants most! His long-lost youth! I stomped my foot and did a little dance of frustration, for I felt abused by my own ignorance. (See how shifty the mind is?) I could have him cut about forty years off my back and then make some basic improvements in my looks. Hell's bells, I could have him make me look like Charles Atlas right down to the toes, and with a face like John Barrymore's. Who wants to be old? Who wants to look like a white prune? Who wants to be weak? Who wants to have piles or hardened arteries? Who wants to break blood vessels in his brain when trying to take a crap? Who wants to go to bed every night thinking that there might not be any morning to wake up to? I'll tell you who. No one on the face of the earth.

Anyone who talks about the satisfying golden sunset years would also justify the loss of his eyesight by telling you how he never gets headaches from reading books any more. Golden sunset years? A leaf turns golden sunset yellow before it drops down into the dog dung.

What happened to my high-minded notion that no one ought to tamper with the proper order of things? I forgot it.

As far as I was concerned, it was settled. As soon as I was able to get out of that john, I was going to have Sadass make me just under thirty years old, with the body of a middle-weight boxer. I would have good teeth, a strong heart, veins like blue ropes under my clear skin, and I would have clean breath. When you get old and begin to rot, you forget how sweet-smelling the young are. That's why the old hate the young. It all comes down to simple envy. The young are rich and the old are poor. Simple as arithmetic. Time will make up for the injustice, but that doesn't help your frame of mind any while you glue your plastic teeth onto your flimsy gums each morning.

They were doing something to each other that I can't bring myself to talk about. I guess maybe I am a little bit of a prude. But did I leave? Nope. I just stood there with a big itch thinking of how it was going to be once I got back to my Efrite friend. The dull eye of one of the women was on me, but without much interest, and who could blame her? It was like she was looking at a fly on the white tile behind me. The task at hand came first for her, anyway. I was swallowing dust and staring.

They worked themselves up to a hot pitch. I felt a tug on my pant leg. I guess I had moved up close to them. The big blond woman had freed one of her arms and was absent-mindedly tugging at my cuff with a strong grip. I'll tell you— it didn't do my frame of mind a favor. You damned old clown, I told myself, but the feeling that everything in life is planned out in advance stayed with me, and all my righteous opinions seemed all the more like straw for the fire in my blood. I suppose you have contempt for me, but remember, you were not in my shoes. Even so, I don't blame you. Looking back on it, actually writing it out like this, makes me feel disgusted too. I don't feel guilty about it, though, for reasons you will shortly be able to figure out for yourself, unless of course you are afflicted with sub-normal intelligence.

Then the other one grabbed my other pant leg. They both looked up at me with a kind of sickening pleading in their piggy eyes, and God help me if I didn't feel like a Johnny-on-the-spot saviour come down to assist young women in distress. So I unbuckled, unzipped, and fell to work, believe what you will, sinking into the soft flab like a torpedoed ship into the sea, funny though it sounds to put it like that, but it's true, for there was a general dimming of the lights, it was hard to get air, I swear strange creatures floated around me, unheard-of things, half bat half dog, and a deep groaning sound that might have been coming from the women though it didn't seem human at all, but did I *care?*—no, I didn't, I just kept going after it hammer and tong, red-ball express, smoking.

There's no need to get into the seamy area of details. I'll say this much: it was a hot trio. What is more interesting, anyway, is the flood of crazy ideas that filled my head as I bulled those two porkies around that rest-room floor. Where I had been lacking in ideas before, a harvest of what seemed like pretty good notions occurred to me. I mean about what to do with Sadass the Efrite. Such as: after I was young and good-looking, I'd move out of my old apartment and get into one of those nice condominiums up in, say, Newport Beach, or maybe in Malibu. I would shed my old-man ways. I would give myself the power to point-and-get. —You there! The one with the honeydew melons in your sweater! Jump in my car, this Cadillac here with the solid-gold radiator grille! Where are we going? My place, girlie, where do you think! And here we are. (The place knocks her eyes out. It's hanging over a canyon, overlooking the city. The view out the other end is of the ocean. The rooms are ninety feet on a side and the carpets are made out of fur. The furniture is silver, gold, carved ivory, and the bed is four feet thick, solid goose feathers. I show her my money chest. It's packed solid with one-thousand-dollar bills. I give her a handful. What is she ready to do? Any damn thing I want!) All right. You're next, blondie. Yes, that's me you hear flying over your head in this helicopter. We've got a date. Forget that moron you're with. We've got a ship waiting for us out in the harbor. She climbs up the rope ladder and off we go. We settle on the deck of my private yacht. Isn't this the bee's knees? Okay, strip down and join the others below. I've got fifty of them waiting for me. Starlets with long blond hair, and we are going to the South Seas. We have a great time. But at an island somewhere between Hawaii and Japan I trade the lot for a load of native girls. One of the abandoned blondes slashes her wrists on a sharp shell in a fit of jealous grieving. Another swims out after the yacht, sobbing among the whitecaps, where she drowns. One thousand, next, in a barn, the smell of hay and manure, and one by one they shudder under my bulling, but it isn't enough because I never get tired, never too pooped to pop, never have to suck wind. Boredom comes into the picture. It gets me irritated. Son of a bitch. I'm sore as hell, ready to kick ass. I don't like the look in the eyes of number nine hundred and ninety-nine. I have her whipped red by number one thousand. And then I take them both while the others applaud. Then we start over at one. I warn them that if I get bored this time there is going to be hell to pay. But I can see—dimly yet, but it's there, like a hand held up on the horizon—*boredom*. It's going to be a problem. I try to ignore the idea. Maybe outright rape will help some. I'm galloping now through the woods outside my castle walls and there's a group of maidens harvesting wild berries. I dismount and remove my gold-plated armor. Hey, don't you run away from me, goddammit! I'm the damned king around here, or maybe you dummies don't know that! Well, you'll know soon enough! One tries to escape, but my men go after her and make her return at gunpoint. These girls are from a convent. Well, that's just too bad, isn't it? They are praying, but I don't mind that—in fact, it kind of excites me to see them kneeling. Even my beard is unmerciful, it's iron wire, and makes them bleed. This is like going up stairs. One step leads to another. It's always boredom that makes you take the next step. The itch keeps you moving. Heroes from a dangerous expedition are eating at my table. Their pretty young wives are with them. They are good-looking women. Their husbands have earned the right to eat with me because they have been so fearless in killing off my enemies. But the evening takes a surprising turn. Sorry, boys, but these wives here are coming with me. My men, stepping out from behind the drapes, take the women away. The young soldiers protest to beat hell and swear blood oaths for revenge, but their wine has been drugged and they can't do a damn thing about it. They stagger around and drop like sprayed fruit flies. I laugh at them, for they are the funniest-looking things I have ever seen. It's all good sport. But the next step calls for blood in quantity. Heads by the hundreds of thousands have to roll. You've got to keep the rabble off your back. Pick a few and torture them publicly. It's the law. I am the law. Every last one of them needs to die screaming my name. Once a week, in every village, carry it out. It goes on like this. Until there is only me spelled in capitals. Me alone in the world standing on top of a stone tower overlooking a lake of congealing blood reflecting ten white suns, for darkness is never allowed to settle on my kingdom. The king finds sleep boring. The king does not need to sleep. The hand upraised on the horizon comes closer. It makes me think. Suddenly I realize that I feel lonely. At the core of my boredom there has always been this loneliness. Looking at the hand out there makes me understand this. But I don't want to understand this. And so I make an island rise up out of the thick red sea, and it obscures the hand. The hand is gone. A ship carries me out to the island. It is a beautiful tropical paradise with fishing villages and small terraced farms. I am wearing the disguise that suits the area best. A rural beggar. The people who give me coins are rewarded with interesting stories. The stories are like fables that hold, in their interesting quilt-work designs, the secrets of creation. Soon I attract a wide and fanatical following. The rulers of the island hear of me and of my interesting stories and they get nervous about it, for what I have to say to the people is a whole lot different than the government's established view of things in general. The royal astrologers have books printed up telling how everything I say is a load of bunkum. But the books don't sell very well. A lot of them wind up in outhouses as toilet paper. Well, pretty soon the government has me carted off to jail. The trial date is set. I am charged with Unlawful Public Theorizing Against The Established Way. The trial is quick, fixed, and I am guilty as charged. The sentence is death by hanging. It's done. My body hangs in a public place for days. Birds pick at my eyes. I'm fly-covered. The rulers of the island throw a week-long celebration and one hundred percent participation is required by law or there will be hell to pay. Then in the middle of the festivities a big blue-white light comes rumbling out of the sky like an express train. It surrounds my body. The big party comes to a grinding halt and people start their groveling. The blue-white light is me and I am the blue-white light. I reveal myself to these ignorant people as their one and only true god. All the doubters, the outright haters, the two-faced, and the scheming are skinned alive publicly but are not allowed to die, for they are required to live in a big shit-filled pit, skinless, with stinging beetles for company, and the sky above them rains down pure yellow piss non-stop twenty-four hours a day. Well, they asked for it.

I wrote that part that way so you could get a feel of what it was I thought while wrestling around with those big women, because they were more like dreams than thoughts, the kind of dreams you have after eating an onion sandwich before going to bed, real *vivid*.

Anyway, they came to a stop. Something snapped in my head as if I'd had a stroke, but I didn't feel sick or anything. I just didn't feel like messing with these two fat women any more. I crawled out of that tangle and pulled up my pants.

Back at the table, Sadass said, "Got to you, did they? I told you not to go in there."

I signaled the waiter for a glass of wine. I ached all over, as if I'd been picking fruit all day. Especially my arms and chest and back. My hands were shaky and my teeth were chattering.

"I felt like I'd been slipped a drug or something," I said. "I had some pretty scary thoughts in there. I acted like a fool. Those women—"

"They aren't women, Ulysses," says Sadass. "They're she-devils. The rotten things you thought about were planted in you by them. You were being tempted, old-timer."

It made sense, but I couldn't believe it. She-devils?

"They wanted you to make poor use of me. But if your thoughts, the things you imagined, went from sort of spicy-pleasant to downright nasty-awful, then you must have let the temptation-dreams come full circle to their logical end. You didn't fight them and they had their own way with you until they just came back on themselves, like a train on a circular track ramming itself. You did good. You beat them at their own game. See, if a fool manages to get hold of an Efrite, he only winds up destroying himself. This is what I meant when I told you about the built-in safeguards. You're ready for anything now, little buddy."

I sipped my wine. "It wasn't my idea for any of that to happen," I mumbled, still shook up. It was half a question, half a statement of fact.

"No, it surely wasn't."

"Well, how come—"

But I didn't need to finish my question. I knew that I had gotten into something serious. Nothing was going to go away easy, and nothing was going to be the same for me ever again. See, that Antoine Galland knew a lot more than I did or ever will about Efrites and the way to go about dealing with them. And I knew from the look on Sadass's face that he knew more than he was willing to tell me. Something was going on that was miles—BLAST!!

(*Here begins notebook 5.* I didn't see the end of 4 coming. I guess I got carried away.)

over my head. I figured I would have to be careful in the future. I didn't want to walk into another john somewhere and have to face a couple of greasy she-devils licking each other on the floor. Once is enough. I guess I could have told Sadass to get out of my life forever, for if what he said about me being his master was really true, he would *have* to go away, wouldn't he? Suppose I told him to go to Timbuktu and stay put under an oleander bush for ten thousand years. Would that do the trick? But now, what about this: suppose I mumbled something in my sleep, made an accidental wish —how would I know that he wouldn't cause it to come true by long distance? He even seemed to know what was on my mind, either from reading it directly or by watching my face. If I said one thing, he could claim that I meant something else. If I said, "Go to Little America and bury yourself under a million tons of ice," he might say, "Listen here, my friend, that isn't what you had in mind at all. I'll tell you what you really had in mind. You want me to move into your apartment and be your right-hand man," like when he stopped me from blowing my brains out. I looked at him. Sure enough, there was that big grin that said it all: he knew exactly what was going through my mind. So I just shrugged and sipped my wine, determined not to do anything but let things happen by themselves without my help. I didn't make this world, and by God I'm not going to start acting like it's my responsibility to make fine adjustments on it. I can hear you saying: That's a damn fancy excuse for hanging on to that Efrite, for no doubt that old rascal knew full well that as long as he had him he also had a trump card against anything the world might deal out to him. Well, think that if you like. It's not true.

The belly dancer started up a new routine after taking time out for a sandwich and a cup of coffee, but this time I wasn't interested. She was just a fat girl trying to make a living by entertaining useless old clucks like me. I liked her for that, but not for the way she threw her weight around in time to the music. I had been wired into something treacherously strange, but now I was unplugged from it. I felt funny. Not like before, though, and not drunk or sick, but split off from everything. If a dead man could see, then this is how he'd feel. I felt like a pair of eyes connected to nothing. I guess I was just bushed. The wine might have had something to do with it. Call it a combination of wine and excitement. (Though you are probably calling it a lot more than that by now.) But whatever it was, I didn't mind it. And it didn't surprise me either. I was getting accustomed to out-of-the-way happenstances. A human being will adapt to almost everything, that's something you can count on.

Back at the apartment, there was an important-looking

envelope stuck in the door. I guess it was put there by a
private messenger service. I took it inside, found my reading
glasses. It was from Harold V. Button, Attorney-at-Law. I
still have it, too.

Dear Mr. Cinder:
Your daughter, Mrs. Perry Nettles, has asked me to represent you in the matter of the disposition of your estate,
attendant upon your expiration. Now, I realize that this
can be an unpleasant subject, but if you only knew how
much unnecessary suffering has been caused by the
thoughtlessness of individuals who neglected to leave a last
will and testament, you would no doubt be the first to act
on behalf of your daughter's interests. (Need I remind you
of the confusion, humiliation, the pain, not to mention the
many acts of forgery, that have been caused by the irre-
sponsibility of the late legendary Howard Hughes through
the apparently mindless failure of providing the rightful
heirs of his estate a simple document dividing said estate
among them?) Being a former businessman yourself and a
loving and responsible father, I'm sure you will agree that
this simple, effortless act of paternal affection is necessary
and right, and that you will not want to delay its execution,
aware, as indeed we all must be, of the vicissitudes of this
life. I have therefore taken it upon myself to draw up a
document which names your daughter, Mrs. Perry (Cinder)
Nettles, as sole heir and beneficiary of your entire estate,
copies of which are enclosed. If you would be kind enough
to sign all three (3) copies and return them to me as soon
as possible by means of the stamped envelope enclosed, the
matter will be disposed of to the general benefit of all
parties concerned. Should you have any questions, I will be

available in my office between the hours of 1:00 and 2:00 p.m. a week from Thursday.

Respectfully yours,

Harold Vernell Button

Attorney-at-Law

I signed the three copies of the will without reading it, stuffed them into the envelope, sealed it, took it out into the hall, and dropped it into the mail chute. Then I went back inside and poured myself a glass of Zinfandel.

Sadass, who had read the lawyer's letter over my shoulder, said, "You must be pretty well off, judging from the tone of that lawyer."

"I guess Lorna thinks I am, anyway. But I sure am not Howard Hughes. All I've got is what you see in this apartment, plus a little nest egg over in the First National."

"Somebody must be keeping tabs on that nest egg. You checked out how much it's worth lately?"

I went back to my desk and took out my bank book. I put my reading glasses back on and thumbed through the dog-eared pages. "Six thousand four hundred and ninety-one dollars and seventy-seven cents, as of the first of last month," I said.

"Nothing to sneeze at."

"It's about the price of a new Chevy," I said.

I felt a little put out. In the past few years Lorna never wrote to me without bringing up my will, or my lack of one. I guess she was right to do it. I guess I was wrong to neglect it. But nobody wants to face up to the fact that everything is going to come to a full stop for them, and writing a will can be a cold reminder. It's dumb, though, to act that way. You've got to be a realist in this real world. Bread on the table is more important than lace on your curtains.

You might be getting the idea that Lorna is a mean-spirited girl. That's not true. She was always a sweet-tempered little kid who took after her mother. She looked like a midget-size version of Emily. She liked to read books and spend her time daydreaming. She didn't do very well in school because of that. She hated what they gave her in school to read. Arithmetic made her cry. Sometimes she would sit on my knee and make up stories about knights in shining armor or captains of the sea. She wanted to be a nurse, then an airline stewardess, then a movie actress, then a dancer. But she wound up being nothing other than a wife, getting married to Perry Nettles when she was only nineteen. If she has become grasping and small, I think you would be safe to lay the blame on Perry Nettles, who strikes me as a niggling man.

I took my wine bottle out to the living room and sat down in the big armchair. I was getting depressed. I saw a vision of myself dead on a bier among the wilted chrysanthemums—it was a vision of Emily, but I just replaced her with me—while strangers stripped my apartment. They pulled out drawers and opened closets. They were relaxed about it. They took their time. I wasn't going to jump up and protest. They knew that.

Here I was, an old man come to be worth the price of a new Chevy to the one person who should have felt differently. When Emily died, Lorna had to be given sleeping pills for nearly a year.

There I was, white as a fish's belly, lying helpless and cold while everything was hauled away. Did I ever live? You'd never know it or care.

I guess you'd have to put all this under the heading of Self-Pity. Well, it had been a long day.

Well, look who's here. It must be Wednesday.

He came in blowing smoke like always. Weldon Holloway. Every Wednesday he comes by for a visit. Figures it's his duty to the old folks. Opens the door a crack and a blue stream of smoke comes in, followed by his fourteen-inch black cigar, followed by his beefy red face. Holloway is the Director and owner of this place. Always has a joke to tell. His joke for today:

There's this farm boy walking down the road in summertime carrying a pig, an anvil, a washtub, and a chicken.

Stop me if you've heard it, Ulysses.

I've heard it, but he'll just tell another old one if I stop him, so I tell him to tell it.

He comes upon this woman working in a field. He says, Lady, how about letting me come up to your house for a drink of water? No way! she says. You might rape me! Rape you? he says. How can I rape you if I'm carrying all this stuff? She says, Well, you could put the pig under the tub, the anvil on top to keep him in, and I could hold the chicken.

Holloway laughs until he doubles over. He breaks a sweat and there are tears in his eyes. He is a farm boy himself. A farm boy trying to make himself look like a Cadillac salesman, purple shirt with a white tie, big baggy blue pants, white belt, white shoes, a Joe Stalin mustache, and hair like Shirley Temple. Big dumb ham-handed galoot, but harmless enough.

Anyway, Sadass sits on the couch across from me and commences to give me a long squinty-eyed look while rubbing his chin, as if he's sizing me up for the first time. "Well, what do you say?" he says.

I didn't have anything to say, and I said so.

"I figured out how we can do it," he says, just as if we were having a conversation about something.

But I didn't ask him what he meant. I didn't care. When you get to feeling depressed, you sort of lose interest in things generally.

"Well, do you want to see her or not?"

I looked at my wrinkled hands, the liver spots on them, and the tremor that had gotten worse lately, and it seemed to me then, in my self-pitying state of mind, that I had been losing things for a long time now. Even my hands seemed to be disappearing. I didn't have anything in my life to hold on to. "Okay," I says. "Let's go, then."

He got up and went into the kitchen and came back with two bottles of good stuff, the best I had in the cupboard. A Cabernet Sauvignon made by a little winery up north. I'd paid seven dollars a bottle for it and was saving it for a rainy day.

"We'll take these along," he says. "You might want to get braced now and then." He put the bottles into a paper sack and we left the apartment. I never saw that apartment again.

We took the bus to the airport and bought ourselves a couple of tickets on a half-empty flight to Las Vegas with money he produced. He gave me the leftover money and I stuffed it into my pockets. I had questions, but they didn't seem important, and I didn't feel up to asking them, anyway. Let things happen the way they want to. That's how I felt. Still do. We took seats in the rear of the jet and buckled the belts. I could see that Sadass was working on something big, because he was sweating foam and passing foul gas. His magic seemed to take a physical toll on him.

"You have to do that?" I asked.

"Do what?"

"Fart like a goddamn horse." Sweat was shining on his face and forming thin lines of foam in the cracks around his

mouth. He might have been running a fever. He looked sick.
I said, "You sick?"

"Yeah. I don't know. Maybe."

"What's wrong?"

"Bad food. Too much of it. But I didn't have any choice.
Got to eat. Much as I can." He was talking in grunts, grinding his teeth between words.

I remembered him calling the world a rotten peach. It
made sense. Why shouldn't it be a rotten peach? Everything
else gets old and rots. Why not the world too? But it wasn't
comfortable to think about, as the plane lurched down the
runway, starting to tilt up into the blue sky, and so I put the
idea of rotten peaches out of my mind and reached down into
the paper sack at our feet and pulled out a bottle.

His swampy farts had heads three seats in front of us turning by the time the plane leveled off. Then they'd see that big
dark face of his shining with sweat and they'd turn back
around fast. No one wanted to antagonize this giant Mexican-
looking breaker of wind. I uncorked the bottle of wine and
took a long pull, but I didn't offer any to Sadass. He didn't
seem interested, anyway. He was busy working on his next
trick.

After only minutes of level flying, the plane began to let
down. That's how close it is to Las Vegas. You stay unbuckled for about twenty minutes. I recorked the bottle and
slipped it into the sack when the red sign came on that told
us to buckle up again.

I wondered why—just for a second—why I was letting
myself get dragged to Las Vegas. Emily sure wasn't there.
And there was nothing in that town for me, either, since I am
not a gambling man or a lover of floor shows, and the desert
is about the homeliest piece of real estate on God's otherwise

green earth. Give old man Cinder orange groves on the sea-coast set against lush mountains.

The vibration began in my teeth, but in another second it was in my arms and legs and hands and feet. I looked at the farting and sweating Sadass. His eyes were closed and his teeth were gritted. Rivers of sweat were pouring off him.

"What the devil are you doing?" I asked him. For I was now no longer indifferent or amused but alarmed.

"Not me," he grunted. "It's the plane."

I bristled. My heart kicked over. "What do you mean, it's the *plane*?"

"Left-hand engine just fell off, chief. We're going down!"

He was yelling at me. He had to yell because the vibration had become a roaring and now all the other passengers were screaming their heads off. Stuff had begun to spill out into the aisle and the stewardess was crawling on her hands and knees. The plane felt like a car sliding out of control on ice. Sadass pointed out the window. The whole left wing was following the departed engine. You could see a big tear forming in the aluminum where it joined the body of the plane. Then it went. So quick, it was like it had just disappeared before your eyes. The whole goddamned wing. Whump, and it was gone, and we started into a flat spin that made everything that wasn't tied down bang into the left side of the plane. Overnight bags, plastic cups, magazines, cigarettes, the stewardess who had been crawling on her hands and knees, a couple of hats, someone's sandwich, a lady's shoe, and hundreds of odds and ends. I held on to my wine with both hands.

I didn't get *too* excited, you see, because I was pretty sure it was just one of Sadass's tricks. And sure enough, he was sweating and gritting his big yellow teeth as if he was trying to lift a piano. His eyes were closed tight, and even though his face was usually leather-brown, it was now bright red with blood pressure.

"Cut it out, Sadass," I says. "You're going to scare these people to death."

"Listen," he hissed through his clenched teeth. "It isn't my doing! This is a honest-to-God catastrophe! Not my doing at all!"

*That* got me excited again. It was convincing. The cabin lights flickered, the red emergency sign was on. I could see the ground below spinning like a record on a turntable and coming up to meet us fast as a freight train. Then the thing Sadass set himself to do began to happen. The plane split off from itself. I don't mean it actually split into two halves. It was more like a double exposure on a snapshot. I saw it first in the face of the woman sitting across the aisle from me. She got blurry. Then she split off from herself. It was sort of like she had a double. It was happening to everyone. And not only to everyone but to every*thing*. Everything multiplied by two. Picture a V in a highway and your car splitting into two cars and one car going left and the other going right and the one on the left hits a tree but the one on the right keeps on going just as if nothing unusual has happened. Well, that's exactly how it was. The plane on the left split off from the plane on the right and for a second you could see the screaming passengers sitting over there, and if you turned slightly, you could see them again in the plane on the right, only they weren't screaming but just sitting calm as anything, as if this was what they had expected all along, no surprises. I looked over at the plane on the left to see if I could see what Sadass and I were doing, but our doubles weren't there. The rear of the plane on the left was empty. No big Mexican-looking passenger and no old man next to him. I touched my face and it was my own single face I touched. Everything was quiet except for the hiss of the perfectly running engines. Nobody was talking. Out the window I could see the plane on the left burning on the desert where it had hit. No survivors. And that was for sure.

"Ah, this is hard, effendi," says Sadass, looking like he was about to grit himself to death.

"I didn't tell you to do anything," I says.

"You said—you felt up to a visit—with—Emily. So—that's —where we are—going."

"Saying isn't asking," I says, feeling smug, though I didn't have any right to feel that way, considering the circumstances I was in.

"All these people—except for you and me—are ghosts. But don't get the—idea that—I caused this wreck. These people —were due. Everything—happens on—schedule."

The plane, just like a normal everyday plane, began to let down. As far as I could tell, we were still over the desert just outside of Las Vegas. The sun was still the same bright desert sun, the sky was still the same gas-flame blue of the desert sky, and the ground had the same gray-white pancake look to it. The plane came down on a long smooth stretch of land, and as we taxied I saw all the usual desert shrubbery whiz past, the mesquite, the tall cactus, the spiky flower trees.

When we stopped, all the ghosts got up and filed slowly out. Sadass and me brought up the rear. Someone outside the plane had rolled up a set of stairs, but I didn't see who. It wasn't blazing hot outside, a comfortable eighty-five or ninety, which is cool for the desert in summertime, and the wind wasn't blowing dust into our eyes. We walked down the steps to the hardpan. All the ghosts were milling around as if they were waiting for somebody to tell them what to do. Then a big black dog the size of a Great Dane but belonging to some breed I'd never seen before trots up to us. It stood there for a few seconds as if it was counting heads. It gave me and Sadass an extra-long look and I felt my own hackles go up, but then it turned and trotted away. All the ghosts followed it, just like they knew they were supposed to.

"Come on," says Sadass. "We got to—hurry it up—this here is—goddamned hard—it's a son of a bitch, chief—to hold—together."

I smelled rotten peaches among the farts. I looked at him. He looked like he was still trying to lift a piano with his teeth while walking on broken glass in his socks. He was also stooped over quite a bit, like an old man himself, and he looked thinner, as if this trick of his was using up his body weight fast. I started to sweat myself, and not because of the desert heat, which, as I said, wasn't all that bad.

The big dog trotted ahead of us, leading the way. We traveled about a mile before we saw where we were headed. There was a big bunch of people, more ghosts, I guessed, standing out on the desert. They seemed to see us coming, but they didn't look especially happy or even interested about the arrival of company.

I started to get a funny feeling I didn't like. A premonition. The ghosts joined the other ghosts and it was like an army standing in a field waiting for orders. There were so many of them that you couldn't count heads. The crowd went on and on as far as you could see, right to the horizon, every direction you turned, except the direction that we had come from. There could have been a million people there. Maybe ten times that. And they all looked pretty much alike. I mean, in the way they dressed and held themselves, like they were all from the same area, such as San Soledad, Los Angeles, and maybe San Francisco. Ordinary people, like you see every day. As we moved into the crowd, I saw what was bothering me about them. Each and every one of those ghosts was not aware of anyone else being around. Eyes didn't meet eyes. Shoulders didn't touch—even though they were packed together. They took the trouble to avoid bumping into each other, but they didn't act as though they saw what it was they were avoiding. You'd go up to somebody and his eyes would just focus on something over your head or over your shoulder or to your left or to your right, and the thing they chose to look at was at least a mile away. They had nice, pleasant expressions on their faces, half smiles, like everything was just fine with them, and there didn't seem to be a nasty customer in the lot. But you could not get them to concentrate on your presence.

We moved through them for a while, Sadass leading the way, until we came to a woman dressed in white. Her back was turned to us, but it was her, all right, and I understood what else had been bothering me about all this. My premonition. For though it was Emily, it was the Emily I knew shortly before she died.

I said, "Emily."

She turned around. She had the same faraway look on her face that all the rest of them had, but when she saw it was me, she took my hand in hers. "Ulysses," she said. "Can you possibly forgive me, dear?" Just like that.

I said, "Forgive you? Forgive you for what?" I felt excited and a little out of control. I noticed that my voice was high-pitched, sort of like when you breathe in helium and then try to talk. I wanted to take her into my arms because the look on her face was starting to break my heart.

"I was not faithful to you, Ulysses," she said. "Neither in body nor in mind. Ulysses, I gave my love to another."

I felt sick. I felt like I was going to heave. I ran away from her and hid behind a big rock. I had the sack with the wine bottles with me and I uncorked the bottle I'd been drinking on and drained it. I wondered if drinking wine was permitted in the hereafter, if that's where this was. I wiped off my mouth on my sleeve. She followed me over to the rock and knelt down beside me. Sadass came too, and I shot him a dirty look. But it didn't register, because he looked like he was about to collapse and die. Emily took my hand in hers. It was not the same hand that touched me earlier that day on the beach. It was an old, thin hand, wrinkled and shaky, like mine. I looked into her eyes. They were sunken in and darker than I remembered them. They were sad and looked genuinely sorry.

"I was weak and self-indulgent, Ulysses," she said, giving me that distant look again. "I despised the orange grove. I wanted to live in an apartment in San Soledad. I wanted to have a social life. When we left Kansas for California, I expected all my girlhood dreams to come true, I expected a life of excitement and glamour. Instead, I found myself on another dirty farm. Far different from any farm in Kansas, but still a farm. I hated it. And then I met Ansel Roe. I fell into the trap I had set for myself."

"Ansel Roe?" I had never heard of any Ansel Roe. I looked over at Sadass, but he wouldn't look back. He was giving the back of his neck a massage and his eyes were closed. "Who the hell is Ansel Roe?" I said.

"Ansel Roe was my lover, Ulysses," said the ghost of my wife. "He lived in that old stucco house on the highway, next to that restaurant called the Hungry Dolphin."

"That is a lie!" I hollered. I ran over to where Sadass had wandered—he looked like a victim of sunstroke—and grabbed his arm. "This is some kind of damned lie you dreamed up," I said. "You're a devil come to needle me in my old age, that's what you are!" He didn't look at me. He was trying to puke. He looked like he was in pain. He walked away from me and sat down on a rock next to a cactus. I followed him but he waved me off like a man about to heave up his guts will. I went back to this so-called Emily.

"I met him grocery shopping, Ulysses," she says. "It happened so surely and quickly that it seemed to me, later, almost inevitable. It *was* inevitable. But that doesn't make me blameless. Do you understand, Ulysses?" She reached out for my hand again, but I wouldn't give it to her. Instead, I uncorked the second bottle of wine and took down a few ounces of it. It tasted like salt water. It tasted like tears.

I didn't believe in any of this, but even so, I felt bitter and vengeful toward her. "No," I said. "I don't understand."

"We do things out of necessity, but that doesn't mean we aren't accountable. Being accountable is also part of the necessity. You see?"

I looked away from her. She wasn't looking at me anyway, but sort of through me and beyond me, as if I was the damned ghost.

"It happened so quickly, Ulysses. Ansel merely touched my arm. He said, 'The honeydews aren't ripe yet, *chéri.*' And something in the tone of his voice and in the pressure of his hand on my elbow made me weaken instantly. Things that had been rigid and secure melted within me at that very moment. It was as if what he said about the honeydew melons was a secret code that only the two of us understood. And when I turned to look at him it was as if I was seeing an old friend for the first time in years. It was like a reunion, Ulysses, even though I had never seen him before in my life."

I wanted to get out of there. But heaven help me, I needed to hear it. I drank the brackish wine and waited.

"He was an artist. A painter. He lived in his little beach house painting marvelous seascapes. He would sing to me.

He had a guitar—you remember how much I loved guitar music?—and he'd play songs that he composed himself. It was wonderful, Ulysses. I went with him to his house on that very first day. He said all he wanted to do was paint pictures of me from that day on to the end of time. I was flattered. It was such a beautiful thing to say. I felt that my life was drab and that the chance for a glamorous existence had passed me by. Then Ansel came and everything changed in an instant. Those all-day shopping trips to San Soledad were really excuses to be with him in his little cottage."

I was in the grip of an agitation that went down into my guts. "We had a good life, Emily! We were good to each other. I loved you. And you loved me, in your way, I know you did!" I guess I was blubbering. Some of the other ghosts were looking at me, or through me, with a look of disapproval and pity on their pale waxy faces. I glared at them, for now I was sure that this place—if it wasn't a slick spot in my brain—this hereafter, wasn't heaven but a place to keep two-faced betrayers and self-serving liars.

I said, "Then you're justifying what you did? Is that what you mean? You couldn't *help* yourself?"

"No. I'm not justifying anything. That's always futile. I'm only telling you how things are over there"—she raised her eyes to the direction we came here from—"in the human world. We are victims of ourselves. It's almost impossible not to be. Ulysses, I never made you suffer. I was always a wife to you."

It made me want to spit. I picked out a flat rock and hit it dead center. "Seems you were a wife to Ansel Roe too," I said, half choked on bile.

"We loved each other. We were in the grip of a deep romantic passion. It made life possible for me."

That was the last straw. I had paid for the clothes she wore on her back, the food she put on the table, and the roof over her head. This Ansel Roe sounded like a bohemian deadbeat good-for-nothing who was probably half starved for the lack of means. She probably bought him groceries too, with my money. "Is that why you're here," I said, "on this empty desert? Because you betrayed me?" I hoped it was.

"Oh, Ulysses," she said, touching my face with her old woman's hand. She looked directly at me then, as if both of us were really there, and God help me but I was glad she was suffering, for I believed she really was.

I stood up and stepped away from her. If I had anything left, it was my memories. Now they were gone too, worthless as yesterday's newspaper.

"I didn't hurt you while I was alive, Ulysses," she said. "I gave you a good home, a good life. I believe I even gave you pleasure. But I also gave Ansel Roe pleasure. Giving pleasure to others is not contemptible. I'm not here for that. I betrayed you only in the sense that I finally betrayed myself. I'm here, in this place, to reflect on what I did to myself in the final years of my life, the mistake I made."

"Did to *yourself*? What did you ever do to yourself beyond making your life as cozy as you could, reading magazines and drinking tea while I looked after the trees!" The other ghosts nearby, who had been eavesdropping, now drifted away. Some of them were shaking their heads glumly, disapproving of me as though I was the one who had been a weak-willed two-timer. I threw my empty wine bottle after them, and it smashed on a rock.

Everything suddenly got warped. A big bend had been put into everything. The ground bowed up so that I was standing on a hill, only all directions were the same, so that the downward slope was anywhere you turned. It seemed like I was starting to fall in several directions at once like the hundred petals of a flower opening wide, wilting, and falling away from the center to be carried away by the wind, and every single dried-up petal was me. Emily was bent too, right across her middle, like a strung bow, and her head got enlarged and drifted to one side on her wavy neck. It was happening to everybody. Sadass came staggering over to me and grabbed my arm. He was shimmering on the edges like Jell-O.

"We—got to—get our—butts out—of here, chief," he says, half strangled with the effort to talk. "I can't—hold it—any more." He was withered and old and barely able to stand up. Inside his shimmering edges he seemed to be shrinking.

"Goodbye, Ulysses," said Emily, her voice sifting through the grainy air like a thread of wind.

I felt bad. "Emily!" I didn't know what to say. I still loved her. Even after what she told me.

"You are partly right, darling," she said. "I was self-indulgent and weak. When Ansel finally discarded me after our many years together, I lost my will to live. That's when I began to die, and if I betrayed you, it was in my refusal to go on living. Ulysses, my sin was spite. I got sick and died for spite and self-pity. In that way I made you suffer. It was malice, Ulysses, and for that I ask your forgiveness. I wanted the world to pay for my loss, and the only world I knew was the one we shared."

She began to splotch and tear. Big holes appeared in her bloating body.

I said, "But you were really sick, Emily! The doctor said so! You had low blood pressure, you had spells!"

"The mind's vengeance against the body, Ulysses, nothing more."

She was fading fast. She was floating away from me, all

distorted, like she was made out of a sheet of rubber that had been stretched too far and was tearing itself apart, and between us there was wind filled with stinging grains of sand. "Forgive, dearest," she said.

I yelled her name again. I said, "Emily, I'm sorry too! What I said—!" But she was gone.

Then something nearly knocked me down. It was Sadass yanking on my arm. "We got to go!" he bellowed. We began to trot away from there in the direction we came from. The big black dog followed us for a ways, muttering to itself like some kind of grousing bureaucrat upset with some irregularity that had been forced on his routine, and then it turned back. I looked for an airplane but didn't see one. I guess it warped out of sight with the rest of them.

We kept moving. The warp that had made everything rubberize was more or less gone, and the desert we were trotting on seemed like the real thing again, flat and gritty. The sun was hotter too, and a sandy wind was blowing. Sadass pulled up beside a fat cactus and sat down in its shade.

After we had caught our breaths, I said, "I just want to say thanks very much for the swell time I didn't ask for." I was being sarcastic.

"Flattery gets you friends, truth gets you enemies," he says.

"I didn't ask for either," I says.

"Well, we're back, that's the important thing."

I couldn't argue with that.

"That there is Las Vegas," he said, pointing. I looked, and sure enough there were the tall white casinos and hotels on the horizon. They were somewhat warped too, but this time it was because of the heat waves rising up off the desert floor. After we rested for about a half an hour, we walked over to the Interstate Highway and hitched a ride with a couple of kids who were driving a van that was covered with ten different kinds of paint slapped on with a trowel.

There's a little bit left to this notebook, but I think I'll quit here. This is enough for one day. I'm tired. I ache. Angina pectoris, they say. The Grim Reaper will scratch at the door from time to time.

You have probably noticed that I have quit saying things like, "You no doubt won't be able to swallow this, but—" and the reason is that if you are still reading this story, you are probably one of those people who will say yes to nearly anything.

I remember Warren Harding's daddy telling him, "Son, if you was a woman, you'd be in the family way *all* the time."

This isn't saying anything against you in particular, whoever you are. Warren Harding was a hell of a nice man.

He was just a lousy President.

# Notebook number 6.

I felt about as bad as Sadass looked, and he looked terrible. If he looked about forty when I first ran into him, he now looked sixty. Sixty with an awful lot of hard mileage to boot. He walked along in a stooped-down shuffle, scuffing along and shaking like he had palsy. But I had my own problems.

Emily was on my mind. Emily and that louse, Ansel Roe, if he was real—which I wasn't ready to believe—and if what happened between them really did happen. So I didn't pay much attention to Sadass, except for noticing he looked half dead, but when he wobbled over to the curb (we were walking in downtown Las Vegas, one street over from the street they call The Strip) and toppled over without a word onto the hood of a pearl-gray Cadillac, passed out cold, I forgot my own troubles for the moment.

I grabbed his shoulder and gave him a shake. But he was out. A few people were looking on: some tourists in short pants taking pictures of what they believed was local color, and some seedy-looking congenital gamblers whose desperate eyes were only temporarily distracted by Sadass's misfortune. All this happened in front of a café called Porky's Chop House. I went inside and asked a waitress if she would mind calling for an ambulance. She said she'd do it right away, and I went back outside to stand guard over my genie, who now looked like he had about as much magical power as a dead stump. His face was as gray as the hood of the Cadillac he had dented. The owner of the car was there too, fretting. He was a little rat-faced man in a white suit, with a dead cigar stuck in the corner of his lipless mouth. He was mad. The dented hood of his car was of more concern to him than the plight of the big sick fellow. He picked up the half-full bottle of wine which had slipped out of Sadass's shirt (he'd been carrying it for me) and lodged itself behind a bumper guard. He looked at it for a full minute, nodding his head the way a man who has had a run of bad luck will (I figured he had just lost the rent money and a car payment or two in one of these casinos), and then set it down carefully on the curb in a kind of comical manner, as if it was a jade vase from ancient China, and all the onlookers had a good laugh over it. Sadass looked like he was on his way to the bone yard to me, but the death of a wino (as most of the onlookers judged him to be) will not ordinarily prevent a bystander from having a good laugh. You can depend on some people enjoying a good joke under most any conditions.

The waitress who I had asked to call an ambulance came out of the café then. "The cops are on the way," she said. I gave her a hard look. Why would anyone want to set the cops on a dying man? But she said, "They're bringing the police ambulance. It's the quickest and cheapest way to get him to a hospital."

I thanked her and dug into my pocket then and there to

give her a tip. I took out the roll of bills that Sadass had produced in the San Soledad airport, and peeled off a ten. I didn't have to do that, but I was sore at that crowd of laughers who took it for granted that Sadass was a deadbeat who deserved to die across the hood of a gray Cadillac in Las Vegas, if only to break up their boredom. I would have told them that this big old boy here was a genuine Efrite, but you know what that would have got me.

But she turned down the money and told me to come on inside for a cup of coffee after the ambulance arrived. I said maybe later. The crowd had become larger and I had to work my way back to Sadass. He hadn't moved a finger. I felt his face and it was cold.

Then the ambulance came screeching up. The two young cops were quick to get Sadass loaded on a stretcher and out of the sun and away from that festive crowd. They asked me some questions. They were friendly boys who seemed to have some understanding of the unexpected trouble that will visit people. I thanked them with genuine feeling, for I am not an ungrateful man when it comes to the important things in this life, such as politeness and respect for a dying man's dignity. They invited me to ride along with them, and I climbed in the back and took a seat next to Sadass. We left the gawkers like a rocket hell-bent for the moon.

The hospital wasn't far away, and they put Sadass in the emergency ward along with some accident victims, and after a few minutes a doctor who looks like a teenager comes over to Sadass and puts his stethoscope to his chest while a nurse takes his blood pressure.

"History of coronary problems? Drug abuse? Dizziness?"

I guess he was asking me, but he couldn't take his eyes off

Sadass, who even half dead and shriveled was a formidable sight.

I said, "Search me, doc. Since I've known him, he's been pretty healthy."

"That I sincerely doubt," he said, taking his stethoscope out of his ears. "Sometimes they'll put up a good show for months, or even years, then drop. They get plenty of warnings, mind you. The body doesn't usually play surprises on you. But most people choose to ignore the little signals, thinking that they can tough it out without professional help. Your friend here strikes me as the sort of rugged type who would never admit to anyone, especially his friends, that he was experiencing adverse symptoms."

It was a little depressing, listening to this peach-fuzz kid talk like the chairman of the board. He looked eighteen, but I suppose he was ten years older than that.

"That might be true, doc," I says, "but if you knew him yourself, you wouldn't think that he could ever have anything go wrong with him like this." I was tempted to tell the kid that he was examining a genie who could turn this hospital into a grove of fruit trees in a split second.

"Tell me something," says Dr. Peach-fuzz. "Did this big fellow ever play football? For the Los Angeles Rams? About twenty-five years ago? Defensive end? He did, didn't he?"

I shrugged.

The doc snapped his fingers. "Hell yes, now I remember. I'm a historian of the game. This is Tyrone Haygood, isn't it? Well, I'll be damned! Tyrone Haygood! The *first* of the quick big men."

I didn't say anything. It was a good story he was handing me. It would explain a lot in a pinch. A big football player. It made sense. Played for the Los Angeles team way back twenty-five years ago, the first of the big quick men. Big rugged fella. Never complained a day in his life about any sickness. Played a game once with a broken neck. Say, you should see him put away a steak! And *eggs*? This big buffalo will put down two dozen fried eggs for a snack.

So, after a few seconds of thinking this all out, I says, "That's him, doc. You're exactly right. This here is Tyrone Haygood."

The doc shook his head like he couldn't believe his good luck. Then, remembering that his hero Tyrone is sick, he got thoughtful. "Hard times, right?" he asks.

I nodded, solemn as a deacon. "Lost all his money in the stock market. Wife died in a car crash. He's been this way, on the bum, ever since."

I fished out a handful of that paper money. "Doc, can you put Tyrone here in a private room? Take extra-good care of him?"

I actually wasn't worried too much about Sadass. I was pretty sure he was just suffering from having produced that business back there on the desert and just needed to get some sleep. But I didn't want him to wake up in a ward with a lot of sick people, for he would no doubt scare half of them into the hereafter with his tricks.

"No problem. We have plenty of space. We wouldn't have if there had been a lot of survivors, but there wasn't anything left out there that could be identified as a body. They've been picking through the mess with tweezers."

This made me catch my breath. I had been half wanting to believe that our little trip into the hereafter with those ghosts had been something that had happened in my head, like in that Greek restaurant, and that it didn't have anything to do with the real world or the real hereafter. *Half* wanting, for I wasn't ready to trade my sanity for reassurance about Emily. Selfish to the end, that's what we are.

I guess I was giving the doc a blank look. "The wreck," he says. "Didn't you hear about it? Flight 659, out of San Soledad. Thirty-one dead, including the crew. Just a few hours ago."

I didn't want to think about it. "Is he going to be all right, doc?" I says, nodding toward Sadass.

"Hard to tell. I can't find anything wrong with him, on the basis of this preliminary exam. Good heartbeat, good respiration. Blood pressure is reasonable. We'll know more after we conduct some tests."

A nurse came in then and asked me to fill out a paper that wanted to know all sorts of things about Sadass. I made up a bunch of stuff about him—his age, his address, names of nearest relatives, and so on—and then went out to get that cup of coffee the woman in Porky's Chop House had offered to me. But by the time my taxi driver got me there (he took about ten times as long as the police ambulance did getting to the hospital from that café), I was in need of more than just coffee.

"The chicken-fried steak," I told the waitress. It was the same one who had asked me in for coffee. "Mashed potatoes, no soup, the Thousand Island on the salad, rolls instead of toast, coffee black."

"Your friend going to make it?" she said, not bothering to write down my order on her pad. She was one of those waitresses who remembers your order. I admire people who take what they do seriously, no matter how simple a job it is.

"Don't know," I said. "He's got sand. But so did the best of them who went and died anyway."

She gave me a funny look, like I had said something a little peculiar. Well, I suppose I had. Considering what had happened to me since I woke up in the park that morning. That morning! Was it possible? Seemed like a year ago.

"Maybe he's just had a little sunstroke," she said, trying to cheer me up, I guess. "You've got to watch yourself out there on a day like this."

She brought me a cup of coffee, some silverware, and a glass of ice water. She was a plump woman whose fat had sort of accumulated in the wrong places, such as her rear end, hips, and jowls, leaving her arms and shoulders more or less average-looking. Her legs were better than average-looking, though. They were long and slender, with a good shape to the knee. You could tell that she was clean and took pride in it. I liked her eyes too. Big soft brown eyes they were, and her breasts were girlishly high. Though large, they did not have any middle-age droop to them.

Such thoughts for a man past seventy.

Before my steak came, I went into the bathroom to wash up. I splashed cool water in my face and rubbed the grit out of my pores and wet down my hair. I combed that thin batch of gray straw with my fingers, then took a good close-up look at myself. I used to be good-looking. My eyes, which once had been clear steel-gray in color, were now milky and dull. My nose, which had always been big, was now too large for my face, which had shrunken in on the bones. The cheekbones stood out like white knobs, and they were webbed with broken blood vessels, blue and purple. I looked at my teeth, and they had gotten long. A woman would have to have been in a desperate way for a number of years before deciding to take a chance on me. But a man is vain to the bitter end.

I ate my steak slowly. When she swished past my table in

her crisp skirts, I watched her. If she caught me watching, she would smile. By the time I finished eating, most of the other eaters had cleared out. She brought me dessert—raspberry cobbler—and an extra cup of coffee for herself. When she sat down and rested her nice breasts on her forearms across that table from me, a dry lump came into my throat. Only a fool will bite off more than he can chew. And an old fool will choke on that portion. But I gave her a penetrating look anyway that had more promise in it than I could deliver on, and I didn't feel a damn bit ridiculous. I was thinking: "Two can play that game, Emily!"

I get sidetracked by things that are happening now. One of the inmates here wandered down onto the beach in his nightshirt. Then he scandalized a group of sunbathers by pulling his nightshirt off. Hell, he didn't even know where he was. He walked down to the waves and began talking to the wind. He explained later that he was greeting the clipper bark *Grapeshot*, which was being sailed by his grandfather. His grandfather was coming to take him out to sea. They had to stick a needle in him to get him to come back. I can hear him down the hall crying like a baby for his grandfather. "Granpa-pee! Gran-pa-pee!"

"I am going to take a well-earned break," she says. (Getting back to that waitress.) "My dogs are barking!" She took a sip of coffee and smiled at me again. Listen: old fool or not, I was sure there was a Western Union message in that smile meant just for me. I spooned into my cobbler. "You won't find better cobbler in Vegas," she said. She laughed then, showing some gold fillings, lowers and uppers. "Of course, this town is not exactly on the map for its raspberry cobbler!"

We had a laugh at that. Even this little café had three one-armed bandits near the door so that you could donate your change on departing. We made that kind of small talk for a while, then she looked at me with a serious expression on her face, and I thought: Here it comes, Ulysses. "You know," she said. "You remind me an awful lot of Rudy."

I counted to five, then took a deep breath. I said, "Rudy who?"

"He was my husband. Rudy Mepps. He was an older man, and I guess he'd be around your age by now. Maybe a shade younger."

I filled my speechless mouth with cobbler. Poured some coffee in after it. Checked the clock on the wall. 5:50. In the front of the café, under the clock, two old ladies were playing the slot machines. The clank and whiz of the machines seemed to be coming out of the message-sending eyes of Mrs. Mepps when I looked at her again. I looked at my thin hand showing its veins and bones and hid it in my lap.

"Of course, Rudy has been gone for a long time. Over twenty years. I was what they used to call a child bride. Rudy was forty-four when we were married, and I was only seventeen. Yet he was handsome and youngish for his age."

"You're as old as your heart," I said, touching my chest.

She laughed. I liked the sound of it. It wasn't one of those half-strangled *hig-higs* you hear coming from a lot of women, but a full-chested open-mouthed snort, with a smoker's wheeze hacking in at the end. "My name is RoyReena," she said, sticking out her hand.

"Ulysses Cinder," I said, giving her hand a big how-do-you-do pump.

She propped her elbows on the table and leaned forward. "It *is* a wonder, though, how much you resemble Rudy."

"A lot of people look like someone else," I said, not exactly meaning to discourage her.

"That's true. But you even have a freckle under your left eye, just like Rudy did."

"That's a liver spot," I said.

She tilted her chin back and guffawed. "Hell! Everybody gets old! That's nothing to be ashamed of!"

I'm letting you in on all this small talk to try to get you to appreciate how simple it is sometimes to find yourself involved in a situation with another person almost by accident, in case you didn't know. Don't get impatient with me. The "situation" is coming up.

I had to laugh at her thinking I was ashamed of being old. I reserve shame for more deliberate acts than that. But I didn't tell her I wasn't. I just joined in laughing as if all my problems were over, and for all I knew they were, for who can tell what such accidental meetings will lead to? Anyway, the upshot of this little conversation over coffee and cobbler was this: she wound up asking me to go to the movies with her that evening, and only because I happened to remind her of her long-gone husband, Rudy Mepps. She explained that she usually went to the movies with her friend Marva Sloane but that Marva was down with summer flu and there was a Robert Redford movie in town and she swore we'd have a good time. A man who says no to an offer like that is already in the grave, regardless of his age. The poison of revenge was also in my heart, but I convinced myself that my purposes were more wholesome than that.

For a movie sounded like a good idea to me. I needed to get my mind off the crazy events of the day, culminating in Sadass's public collapse. I was glad to be rid of him for a while. I didn't plan to check on him until the next morning, if even then. I'll admit I had gotten to like him somewhat, but when it comes right down to a man's real self-interest, a genie is something he can do without. Maybe this sounds hard-hearted to you. Maybe so. But he wasn't exactly my nephew, now, was he?

RoyReena's shift ended at six. I had another cup of coffee while I waited for her, and then we took the bus to her place, which was a double-wide Kit Karson parked in a mobile-home court called Sand Hill Vistas. I watched TV in her front room while she got ready. Then we went to the movies downtown. We took a cab. I wanted to pay for it, but she wouldn't let me. She paid for the movie too.

After that, we went back to her place and she fixed us some drinks. She took off her shoes and whizzed around her kitchen as swift and businesslike as she had been in the café. She made a rum and Coke for herself and gave me some sherry, which was the only wine she had on hand. We sat on the couch and listened to her Lawrence Welk records, which she believed I would enjoy. Her personal favorite was Eddy Arnold, but she said she'd put those records on later. I said it didn't much matter to me, since I didn't like modern music anyway. Whatever happened to the simple old songs like "Genevieve," "Sweet Adeline," "Girl of My Dreams," or that real floor stomper, "Captain Jinx"?

She got a little tipsy. She told me her life story. I didn't mind. It's one thing to listen to some miserable wino tell you the confused and falsified history of his worthless life, but a sweet-smelling waitress is another matter. Here's what she told me, more or less as I remember it:

"I was a waitress way back then when I met Rudy Mepps. Just a shy little baby of seventeen is what I was, fresh out of high school. I worked as a carhop in the Arctic Circle outside of Priest River, Idaho. Rudy drove in with the fanciest car I had ever seen. It was one of those Kaiser-Frazers that looked like it came out of the Buck Rogers comic strip, all blue with a silver top and whitewall tires. It looked like it was going sixty even while it was parked! And Rudy didn't waste any time either when I brought him his cheeseburger and strawberry shake. He grabbed my wrist—not in a mean way, but nice and soft—and he asked me if I wanted to go for a spin after work that night. I could hardly keep from yanking off my apron then and there and climbing in the front seat next to him! I didn't have a very good home life—my dad had left to prospect for uranium in Montana, at least that's what he said, and my mama started to run with a crowd of rowdy drinkers. When it was clear that there wasn't any uranium in Montana and that my dad had just used that story so he could pull up stakes for good, Mama let a couple of her rowdy friends move into our house. I hated that. Sometimes a drunken logger would come scraping at my bedroom door in the middle of the night. I was often terrified. So when Rudy said, Let's just keep on going! I said, Okay! just like that, and we drove all the way to Salt Lake City that very night. But Rudy was a gentleman. I want you to know that. He didn't try to ruin me. We took separate rooms at a twelve-dollar motel and he paid for them out of his own pocket. Rudy was a farm-equipment salesman and had just sold two top-of-the-line combines to a big corporate farm in eastern Washington and he had a lot of money in commissions. He said he was going to take himself a little vacation and have a little fun for a change. I am tired of work work work, he said, and he told me I was welcome to ride along without 'obligation,' if I understood what he meant, and though I was just a baby, I said I did. It was true. Not once did Rudy attempt to have his way with me. I almost felt a little pouty because he didn't even try to kiss me or put his arm around me. After Salt Lake we came to Las Vegas. Rudy said, Just look at this shining city, it is really going to be something in the coming years, and will you marry me, sweetheart, so that we can enjoy it together? It knocked me down! Out of a clear blue sky, Will you marry me, sweetheart! But he was serious. He wanted to settle down with a good clean girl in a fine town like this before life passed him by. Rudy was obsessed with the idea that life might pass him by. He often said he felt like a stranger in a train station watching the Super Chief pull out without him, and he called that Super Chief 'life.' He said he had a good job offer from a business-machine company. He said he was sick and tired of selling implements to tightwad farmers and only occasionally hitting the jackpot with some big outfit like those corporate farms. He said he was ready to wear a suit, vest, white shirt, and tie and deal with real honest-to-God businessmen in their air-conditioned offices. Rudy had beautiful fingernails—strong, you know, not bendy and brittle like mine—and, oh, he *did* take good care of them, always clean, always trimmed. Honest-to-God businessmen like to see decent nails on a man, he said. Well, I was just swept away with it all. I didn't have a single reason to exclude myself from his plans. What girl in my situation would? There was nothing for me back in Priest River. I had already sent Mama a post card from Salt Lake telling her I had left Priest River, but I knew she wouldn't care, and that she was probably glad to have me out of the house so she could move in some more of her trashy friends. So Rudy and I got married. That was twenty-two years ago. I was in love for the first time in my life, or at least I thought I was, because what does a seventeen-year-old infant know about love? As a matter of fact, what does a forty-year-old know about it? It's mystery number-one in my book. I don't want to get too personal, but you're a mature man who has probably seen an awful lot of foolishness, so you won't mind if I go into some detail. Sometimes if you talk a thing out to a stranger you get a better understanding of it than if you just keep turning it over and over in your own mind. Well, we moved into a trailer court, not as fancy as this one, but nice enough. We rented a nice single-wide that had a kitchenette and two bedrooms. You could grow flowers outside in a box if you wanted to, but no pets or children allowed, they were strict on that. It had a swamp cooler instead of a real air-conditioner, but I didn't mind the heat when I was young. Now of course I have to have refrigerated air. This will happen as you grow older. This country is suited for kids and lizards, period. Rudy wanted to sleep in separate bedrooms. Too hot for two people to share a bed. This is what he said. I could not believe it! I was heartbroken. I was a young girl in love. I was pure, you understand, but I still knew the facts of life. Rudy explained that things would work out and that nature would take its own course in good time without our rushing things along. I would lie in bed watching the lightning storms flare against the mountains. We have years to get used to each other, he said. I said I understood, but I didn't. Then one night, after about two weeks of sleeping alone, I went into his bedroom. I could tell he was only pretending to be asleep. He was lying with his face turned to the wall, and not even breathing so you could hear him, as if that's how a man would sleep! I got into bed next to him anyway. I am someone who will take a bull by the horns. It's my way. In my high-school yearbook they named me The Girl Most Likely to Speak Her Mind. That's me, all right. As you can probably tell! Well, hold on another minute. It was no big deal. I just wanted to point out that even though he was a terrific salesman to the world at large and deathly afraid that the world was going to pass him by, to me he was just a great big shy baby, shiest thing I ever laid eyes on. That was quite a night. Funny, sort of. I can laugh about it now. Him pretending to sleep, me rubbing up against him like a hot little heifer against a post—whoops! Must be this rum and Coke! I don't mean to get too personal. But he kept on pretending to be asleep. He even started in to snore. Snore snore snore! But I knew it was a big fake. Because his thing was big as a cucumber and hot as a bulb. Oh dear, am I talking dirty? Rum! Can you forgive me, Ulysses? I must be drunk. This mouth of mine! Get her boozy and she's a floozy. Oh well. I just wanted to give you some idea of how crazy people are in general. Well, you're a mature man who has seen a lot and I'm probably not telling you anything you haven't heard a dozen times before. Just go ahead and tell me to shut up when you've heard enough, okay? I won't get mad. I like a man speaking his mind. Just speak up. Put me in my place. I do run on. I know I get to chattering like a monkey. It's Marva's pet peeve about me. Talk talk talk. Hey, slow down, RoyReena, Marva will say. Where was I. Oh. Anyway, there I was, a baby of seventeen, pushing this so-called sleeping man over onto his back and then climbing up on top of him and trying to get everything done all by myself even though I didn't know up from down and so forth. Yet that is exactly how we became man and wife, him pretending to be dead to the world and me pushing myself down on that hot cucumber of his until I found the right place. Isn't that a laugh? Say, isn't that the darndest thing? Probably not. A man such as yourself has probably heard of crazier things. We did it that way all the time, Ulysses, and poor old dumbbell me didn't think there was anything especially peculiar about it. Pushing a shopping cart around the Safeway store, I would look at the other wives and think that they were all doing it the same way with their husbands. I pictured all Las Vegas asleep at night, just the men that is, and them only pretending at that—snore! snore!—while all these wives were working those fifty thousand hot cucumbers—give or take a few—into the right places. What a nut! But I don't want to bore you with the details. You've heard it all already, a man of your years, from A to Z. The main thing I wanted to tell you about was what happened to us after the first few months of married life. The queerest thing about marriage is not what goes on between the sheets but what it brings out in each party's personality. It will bring out things you never suspected were there. I'm still amazed just to think about it. Rudy was a well-liked man. That sounds simple enough, doesn't it? Perfectly harmless. It's good to be well liked, isn't it? You'd think so. But to me, at the time, it was nothing of the sort. That little feature in our lives brought out something in me that I find a little scary, even to this day. It was *jealousy*. Bitter spiteful bitch-dog jealousy. Everybody loved Rudy, and I couldn't stand it! Isn't that awful? We would go to someone's house to play cards or Clue and you could see people just feeling better and better because Rudy was there. I felt as if I did not even *exist*. Rudy this and Rudy that! Men got him into the kitchen to talk over business. Wives made over him, bringing him coffee when he didn't need it or trying to push another piece of pie or cake on him when he was full. And me, I'd just sit over in a corner staring at my nails, which I had bitten down to the nubs. I knew it had to do with me being so young, only seventeen years old, and his friends all being around his age. But I hated it. I'd meet a mutual acquaintance in Safeway or Sears and the first thing they'd want to know about was Rudy, good old Rudy. Me? They couldn't have cared less! That's how I felt, anyway. It filled me with evil thoughts. I pictured myself saying things against Rudy. Such as, Rudy despises crippled-up people and drops lead slugs into March of Dimes cans. Rudy has always cheated on his income taxes. Rudy never buys me anything nice. Rudy voted for Stevenson. Rudy spends the grocery money in the casinos. And so on. Of course I never said any of those things. But the evil thoughts ate away on me like a poison. I got bitter and moodier by the day. I stopped going to his bedroom every night. Or when I did go, I'd just lay beside him for hours sometimes, pretending to be asleep just like him, knowing that he was going crazy waiting for my hands even though he himself stayed quiet as a corpse. And when I did get on top of him, I would treat him rough, as if it was just a dead inanimate thing without any feeling in it that I was using on myself for my gratification alone. I would hurt him a little by my rough ways and he would yip like a puppy under his fake snoring. I guess I was sick in the head with jealousy. I wanted to be well liked too. But his friends only treated me like I was something that stood in the way of their affection for Mr. Nice Guy Rudy Mepps. Oh, they were polite! They tolerated me! They would ask me how things were going for the new bride. You know what I mean. The things you say when you can't think of anything else to say because you basically don't care a whole lot, like when you talk to a child. That kind of politeness can sour cream soda. Rudy began to notice that there was something going wrong between us. I had climbed up on my high horse and his name was Spite. Oh, I had become a regular Queen of Sheba who had been mistreated. I sent him on fool's errands to make him prove that his love for me came first. I'd get him out of the house at two in the morning for a pizza. No, I was not in the family way. I'd go downtown and make him meet me for lunch even though his schedule was nearly always full. I made that man jump through hoops, one test of his love after another. But it was like I was testing the strength of a butterfly with a hammer. I even made him take me to a Mormon doctor in St. George for a checkup without giving him a single reason why. I did it just to bedevil him, and more than once too. Finally, after a couple of months of this, he said, RoyReena, we have to talk. We talked. I broke down and cried. I confessed to him how jealous I had become and how I couldn't stand to be unliked while he was so popular with everyone we knew. Even complete strangers would strike up a conversation with him, while treating me as if I was invisible. Well, he started to laugh it off, but, Sweet Jesus forgive me, I slapped his face as hard as I could to bring him up short. At least he knew then that it was a serious subject and not something to have a good laugh about and by laughing at it make it seem unimportant. I was not in a little 'snit.' I was half crazy. I told him that I knew I was in the wrong but also that I couldn't help myself. Well, what do you want to do about it, honey? he said. He was so nice to me! Here I had just slapped him hard enough across the face to make his nose trickle a little blood and he was still calling me honey! No wonder everyone liked him! He was *likable*! He respected my lack of years. He never once talked down to me, but at the same time he had a lot of patience whenever I tended to babble on and on like the teenager I was. I would sit on his knee and babble. But he never acted bored or superior. Babble babble babble! So when he asked me what I wanted to do about it, I said, I want you to pay more attention to me when we are with your friends. I want you to ignore your friends at parties when they try to get you all to themselves. I want you to say, Let's get RoyReena in here! I want you to sit beside me and talk, just as if I had something really interesting to say for once. Well, that got to him, Ulysses. More than the slap. He didn't like what I was saying. Not a bit. Everyone has a weak spot. Rudy's weak spot was his need to be liked by his friends. And now here was me, a snot-nosed brat from Idaho, telling him that he would have to give up all that, or at least a lot of it, if he wanted me to be happy. That was some choice I was giving him! But I didn't back down. The girl most likely to speak her mind kept on speaking her mind even though it was filled with destructive evil. I would visit his bedroom once a week if he was lucky, and then I was rough on him. I would sit down on him and not move for minutes or until I heard his back teeth grinding, or I would just get it over with with a minimum of fuss. I cooked only the kinds of food I liked best and skipped his favorites altogether. Sometimes I stayed out shopping for clothes and didn't cook dinner at all. Once I flirted with a sailor boy who was on a weekend pass. Nothing happened, but I brought home the silver ID bracelet he gave me and let Rudy stew about it. It was grim around that little trailer house. But my bratty little effort began to get results. He began to give in to me. Party after party, Rudy was not himself. He would drink too much. He seemed remote or sullen, and people began to leave him alone after failing to draw him out on one subject or another. Even the doting women stopped their everlasting doting. Did I understand the damage I was accomplishing? No, I did not! Rudy, who had always been a live wire and an optimist in everything, was now bitter and untalkative. I had infected him with spite. Spite begets spite, as everyone knows, everyone except snot-nosed brats from Priest River. I was too dumb to undo the damage, or even to realize how serious the damage was. I guess I thought I had won something. Won what, I wonder. Nobody wins in the battle of the sexes. We stopped going to parties. Rudy's sales dropped off. He wouldn't shave for days on end. He even neglected his beautiful nails. He'd sometimes not go to work and just mope around the house. He was beginning to act as though life *had* finally managed to pass him by. The train had pulled out without him and the tracks were empty. I won, but it was an empty victory. The trouble was this: I was just too young for him. May can't marry December, but it isn't always December's fault, like people would have you believe. Things went from bad to worse. And I just let them go, thinking that I had achieved some kind of milestone in our marriage. What an ignorant fool I was! Rudy took to drinking. The money stopped coming in, and Rudy had always made good money. I stopped going to his bedroom altogether because even though I had won and was now willing to give him the kind of treatment in bed he had gotten accustomed to earlier, I couldn't stand being close to him now that he had changed. The one time I did go in, he wouldn't respond to me. I fooled around with him, but he stank of liquor and his face was rough with a week's worth of whiskers. I went back into my room beginning to realize finally that I had ruined my wonderful marriage. I promised myself that I would put things right again. I planned a party. But first I would tell Rudy that I wanted everything to be exactly like it was before I made him change. I wanted him to enjoy his friends and his friends to enjoy him without any thought of including me, for I finally realized I was only seventeen and what I had to say wasn't what they wanted to hear, and that it was only proper for things to be that way. I needed a few years to grow up, maybe more than a few years, before I could expect equal treatment. The morning I was going to tell him all this was going to be special. I fixed him his favorite breakfast, bacon, eggs, and dollar pancakes, and then went into his bedroom to serve it to him. But he was gone. His bed was made neat as could be, and there was a note on it that said, I hope you are happy, honey. I dropped the tray and ran outside with tears streaming down my face, and sure enough, the Kaiser-Frazer was gone. I never saw him again. I contacted his friends, but they didn't know where he was either. My heart was broken, Ulysses! I finally understood that I had destroyed the very thing that I loved and needed most in this life, all because of a juvenile pride, and that a second chance is as rare as a jackpot on a dollar machine. I was desperate for months after that and even thought of killing myself by jumping in front of a truck or bus, leaving behind a tragic note that would get printed up in the newspapers and that he would eventually get to read and it would break his heart. I even went so far as to consider going home to Priest River and asking Mama to take me back. But I didn't. Somehow I hung on and stuck it out, finally managing to convince myself that my life was still ahead of me. I got the job at Porky's, where I've been ever since. That is why you gave me such a start when I saw you with your sick friend today. I thought you were Rudy Mepps, come home after twenty-two years. It was a shock."

Her eyes were misty. We were both a little bit stinko. I had finished over half of that bottle of sherry, and she was working on her third rum and Coke. She went to the record player and put on an Eddy Arnold record. When the music came on, she started to waltz around the small front room of the trailer house with her eyes shut and the ice in her glass tinkling. I wondered if this was the same trailer house she'd shared with Rudy Mepps during those few months of her married life. But then I remembered that the first trailer was a single-wide, and this was a double. She was wearing a green dress that was drawn tight around her knees, and as she waltzed, it hiked up on her. After a few turns around the room, it was halfway up her pink thighs. I had some reckless thoughts right then.

This is the end of notebook number 6.

Let me just add what was going on in my mind, though,

while she told me of her mistake with Mepps. A rhyme we used to throw at each other when we were in grade school:

> *Oh, what's the use*
> *Of chewing tobacco*
> *And spitting the juice?*

That make sense to you? Makes sense to me. Sixty years later.

Seven. "You going to let me dance all alone, Rudy?" she says, just barely murmuring, but I heard it all right. Her eyes were still closed. I figured she was drunk and maybe a little crazy to boot. At any rate, I didn't remind her that Rudy had cleared out twenty-two years ago or that my name was Ulysses Cinder. Instead, I set my sherry down and got up off the couch. When her room-circling dance brought her to me, I reached out and took her by the wrist the way Rudy had done when he took her away from that drive-in in Idaho. She pressed right up against me and put her arms around my neck. This brought my face into her hair at neck level. Her smell was extra nice up close, and her high, wide, and handsome breasts took me in, the way the arms of a child would take in a puppy. I got all stirred up, and her thighs aggravated my condition. She took notice of that and opened her eyes for a second to give me a sleepy look of surprise, and then she hugged me closer.

Now exercise and excitement of that kind are not in order for a man over seventy with a bad pump. A fairly strong pain flared up across my chest. It made me hang on to her for support. There were bright spots like weightless airborne diamonds in front of my eyes. So when Eddy Arnold quit singing I was grateful. I sat back down on the couch and tried to take in air.

"You look out on your feet," she said, but she didn't call me Rudy.

"I think I need to lie down," I said.

She knelt down and looked at me with an expression on her face that told me more than I wanted, just then, to know: I am not going to beg, but everything a man could ever want is right here in this double-wide Kit Karson tonight, and what I would like to know right now is, can you fill the bill, old-timer? Eyes, unlike words, always get right to the point.

I said, "Mrs. Mepps, I don't feel too good." All my ideas about getting a little revenge on Emily were long gone.

"I want you to call me RoyReena," she said, undoing my belt. With my belt undone, it was easier to breathe. Then she unlaced my shoes and slipped them off. "Come on," she said. "I'll help you into the spare bedroom. You're just worn out from having a bad day, your friend taking sick and all."

"Oh, wait, now," I said. "There's no need—"

She touched my cheek. "Jesus love you for a martyr, but there *is* a need," she said, sort of scolding me as if for thick-headedness, but gently.

She pulled me up off the couch. She was a strong woman from years of packing dish-heavy trays around Porky's, and I realized that she was going to have her way with me if it killed me or not, and to tell you the truth, I didn't feel all that put out about it, for even though my mortal life was at stake, my natural male vanity was so pleased with the seriousness of her interest that it would have forced me to do handstands if she said the sight of a nimble man got her excited. It was a small bedroom with a Hollywood bed in it and a small chest of drawers. She peeled the bed open, and while I sat on the edge of it, she pulled off the rest of my clothes, leaving me in my underwear, which embarrassed me somewhat because they were a bit stained. When you get old, you develop uncontrollable leaks in your plumbing.

"Now climb in there and have a good rest," she said. "I want to clean up the kitchen and then have myself a nice bubble bath." She lingered in the doorway, holding that promise-of-things-to-come look in her eyes for a few seconds before she switched off the light.

I lay there in the dark listening to my pump and taking deep regular breaths, trying to get it to beat normally. The chest pain came and went, came and went, almost in time with my heartbeat or breathing, but slower, like it had its own schedule to keep and would have nothing to do with the pace of my vital organs. After a while the pains died down, and then came a long stretch of no pain at all, and I didn't move or even close my eyes, for fear of disturbing the truce. And then, without even realizing I was sleepy, I fell asleep. I had a dream. A horse with crazy eyes chased me down a street. It kept trying to bite my hand. I kept slapping at it, but it finally caught the thin skin on the back of my right hand and bit like hell. But I escaped from it and entered someone's house. Damned if that insane horse didn't follow me inside. I jumped out a window, intending to lock him inside the house, but I forgot the back door, which was wide open, and he caught up with me again as I was looking for a hiding place in the attached garage. I was suddenly so scared I couldn't breathe. I woke up. RoyReena was straddling me.

"You're not a burly man any more," she said. "Jesus love you but you're not a burly man any more at all." She was fiddling with me. (Like Vi did yesterday. I was getting my massage, for I was truly bound up, and as she worked down from my belly, her hand sort of slipped and she latched on to me. I jumped. She acted surprised but didn't let go. "Like me to tickle your pickle?" she said. I was so surprised I couldn't talk. She wiggled it for a minute, whistling notes to a song she was making up as she went along, acting all the while as if this was all recognized professional procedure. I wasn't about to complain about it, though, and when she was done she went about her business as usual. I guess it was her idea of a joke.) She was hot and oily from her bath (RoyReena now), and the smell on her was strong. It made me want to sneeze. I rubbed at my nose. If she was looking for a hot cucumber, she wasn't having much luck.

"No, I'm not a burly man any more," I said. "I once was a fairly burly man, but now I'm old."

She broke into a fit of crying. "I'll never be happy," she said. She rolled off me and pulled a pillow over her face to muffle her loud crying. I put my hand on her belly, for I truly liked her. I believed I understood the sadness of her life. "You're a good girl," I said. "And if that Rudy Mepps wasn't man enough to see you through your growing pains, then he never deserved you in the first place."

She came out from under her pillow and raised herself up on her elbows. She stared straight ahead with big wet eyes that didn't focus on anything but took in her unhappiness, which consisted of everything out there that human eyes could see. "There is no Rudy Mepps, Ulysses," she said. "I made him up. Mepps is the only name I've ever had. I've never been to Priest River. I'm a local product and I've never had a man in my life. Not a man I wasn't ashamed to be seen with in daylight, anyway. I have an ugly body and my teeth are bad."

I sat up, gathering the bedclothes around me. The normal human mind is not nimble enough to handle pointless deceit.

So I said, "But Rudy Mepps is the *reason* you're so unhappy."

"I told you there is no Rudy Mepps," she said. "I just invented him to get you worked up, especially the part about me having to climb up on top of him and being too dumb at the time to know that the man is supposed to do all the climbing. Rudy Mepps is not the reason I'm unhappy. I've been unhappy ever since day one. I guess I was born for it." She started crying again. I didn't know what to do, I patted her belly some more, then rested my hand on it. It was jumping in little spasms as she snuffled and sobbed, hiccupped and burped. I felt sorry for her and sincerely wished life had given her a better shake, forgetting for the moment that my own life had pretty much come to nothing after years of thinking it had been better than most.

"Why don't you tell me what really happened to you," I said, as if what happens inside your head isn't as real as most anything that happens outside of it. Maybe that's not a smart thing to say to another person, because it's another way of biting off more than you can chew, but I felt ready to listen to her true story, if not do any climbing.

"Nothing happened to me," she said, between hiccups. "That's the point. I've been working in Porky's for these twenty-two years, waiting for something good to happen to me, but it just hasn't. That's my story from A to Z. I watch TV. I go to movies with Marva Sloane—another loser. Time goes by, Ulysses. Jesus, but it does."

Well, I wasn't going to twist her arm. People who think nothing has ever happened to them are doing a good job of walking through their lives with their eyes shut.

She got up and went out of the room for a few minutes. When she came back, she was carrying a fresh bottle of sherry for me and a big glass of rum and Coke for herself. I sipped the sherry straight out of the bottle. She drank up her rum Coke in a few big gulps. We didn't talk. She had run out of words. There were some words circulating around in my head, but they weren't willing to be aired. Then she got up. "You have a good sleep," she said. "I'll have a nice breakfast for you in the morning."

I sat there for a while, sipping that syrupy stuff and thinking about nothing. It isn't easy to think about nothing. The mind wasn't made to do that. Not for long, anyway. But my head was empty. It worried me. Worrying is a common way of thinking words, but this was wordless worrying. And then it went away too. It was just a mote of dust in a big empty room, passing through a beam of sunlight, and gone. It wasn't natural. Somewhere a weak voice in my head was yelling out loud for me to get up on my feet and get out of that trailer house, for something bad was surely about to happen. But the voice came from across a Grand Canyon and it was too weak to really get me roused. I knew that I should have been scared, and I guess I was scared, but even my fear seemed a faraway thing getting farther away with each breath I took in. Then I watched the sherry bottle laying in front of me slowly emptying itself on the blankets. I felt it wet my legs. I saw my hand reach out for it. That's the last thing I saw that night.

I woke up in a cage with an awful headache. The headache was so bad that finding myself in a small wire cage was only of minor importance at the moment. The cage was one of those kennels for big dogs, all heavy-gauge wire rods, not tall enough for a man to stand up in but plenty long enough to lie down in. She'd put a mat on the floor, a cot-size mattress I guess, along with a pillow. It was in her bedroom, in a corner, away from the windows, which were too high up to reach anyway. She had put a covered plate of food inside the cage. It held biscuits, some link sausages—cold—and a couple of hard-boiled eggs. There was a two-quart thermos filled with coffee next to the plate of food. There was a note Scotch-taped to the thermos:

Rudy:
I'm so happy you have come back, darling. I have always loved you so. I have always known you would. I thought I would never be a happy girl ever again. But now it's all going to be different.

RoyReena

There was a bedpan in one corner of the cage and a roll of toilet paper. There was a bunch of magazines. Today's newspaper. A deck of cards. Well, she was thoughtful, at least.

I didn't get mad. My head hurt too much for that. I guess she had slipped some sleeping pills into that bottle of sherry. I tried hollering for her, but I was pretty sure she had gone to work. The clock radio said 9:45. Her bed was made nice and tight, and the room was clean and fresh-smelling. Sunlight was pouring in through the small windows, making big yellow squares on the opposite wall, which was covered with a flowery wallpaper. The flowers looked like photographs of flowers, and the sunlight coming in on them made them look real. It was like looking out across a field of wild flowers in blazing sunlight. She had taken my shorts off, and I sat there on that pad staring at those flowers like some kind of naked Hindu monk, wishing she'd thought of putting a bottle of aspirins in the cage too.

I have come to believe that every third person or so in the world is stark-staring crazy.

And maybe that is too conservative of an estimate.

I took a look at the kennel's door. It was latched from the outside and the wire-rod bars were too close to each other for even my skinny hand to slip between them. I tried to bend a pair of them apart, but they were too stiff. Wire rods that could be bent by the hands of an old man could be crushed in the jaws of a big dog.

So there was nothing to do but relax and wait for her to come back and hope she was able to listen to reason. I poured myself a cup of coffee, ate a biscuit and a sausage, then laid down on the mat, which was pretty comfortable at that, and hoped that my headache would start going away.

It did. Somewhat. And I dozed off. When I woke up, I felt better. It must have been early afternoon, but I couldn't be sure, for the sun had crawled down to the clock radio, which was sitting on the bottom shelf of a night table, and the clock's face was a miniature sun itself, blinding me when I tried to read it.

I got mad. I hollered. "Damn your fat ass, RoyReena!" I rattled my cage. I yelled, "Help! Help! I'm trapped inside this trailer!" hoping that a neighbor would hear me and investigate. But this was a mobile-home court for working people mainly and was probably pretty much of a ghost town this time of day. Even so, I yelled until my voice gave out. Then I had another cup of coffee and tried to think in a calm way about what that crazy waitress was up to.

Well, it seemed easy enough: she wanted herself a man, *bad*, and she believed that the only way a dumpy middle-aged gal like herself could get one, and get him to stay, was to lock him up in a dog cage and name him Rudy Mepps. I just happened to come along when her plan was ripe. And I just happened to look like the man she had been inventing during all those lonely years of table waiting in Porky's. That made sense to me, if it's ever possible for such things to make sense at all.

It was a long afternoon. I played a few dozen games of solitaire, tried to read a magazine article about the divorce rate in China, ate a couple of biscuits, tried to nap again but couldn't make myself drop off, and then made an escape plan. I would throw a cup of coffee on the clock radio, which was about seven feet away, and short out the wiring for this bedroom. Maybe I'd get an electrical fire started. Then the fire trucks would rush over here and find me. Find me dead or half dead from breathing smoke. I scratched that idea.

I thought about Sadass. I wondered if he could get me out of that cage by long distance. So I said, "Sadass, if you can read my mind, how about getting me out of here?" But nothing happened. Either he couldn't read minds or he was still out cold.

I thought about Emily, and how my dumb notion to get even with her had got me locked up in a cage. How do you get even with the dead, anyway? My stupidity was a thing to behold. Well, I got what I deserved, I guess. Like they say, there's no fool like an old one. If you are looking forward to your old age as a time of wisdom, then you're in for a disappointment. If you're dumb, then you're dumb, twenty or eighty. What sometimes makes an old man look wise is only the failure of his ossified brains to supply his mouth with the usual stupid remark he'd been famous for in the past. So he seems to be pondering. He's not pondering. He's just gone numb between the ears. Sure, there are wise old men. But they weren't well known as dimwits when they were young men, either.

The old boy who was crying "Gran-pa-pee" all night long died this morning. Vi said the last thing he said was, "I'm not even wet!" He said it three times out loud, and his eyes were popped wide-open in amazement as if it was the most surprising turn of events since the Pope admitted that the world went around the sun instead of vice versa.

When RoyReena finally came home, I decided not to let her have it with both barrels but to just sit still like the first move was hers, which it was. But she didn't make it. She puttered around in the kitchen for a while—taking pots and dishes out of the dishwasher and putting them away in the cupboards—then she went into the front room to put a record on her machine. Eddy Arnold again, this time singing "Make the World Go Away." Fine by me, Eddy. After about an hour she came into the bedroom. She didn't look at me. Not once. She acted like that cage wasn't even there. She acted like she hadn't fed a man sleeping pills and locked him up naked in a dog cage. She acted like she and no one else she knew could ever do such a thing. Only a nut would do a thing like that. Bustling around just like she was sane. But she also looked a little bit embarrassed about everything. You could tell she was forcing herself to look "normal." She moved around in a stiff unnatural way and her whistling was a little too loud and the song too cheerful. So I guess she wasn't all that crazy. To be embarrassed about what you've done is a sign of mental health. Her embarrassment didn't include her big undraped body, though, for she shed her clothes right in front of me as if my eyes were glass imitations of eyes. Then she put on her shower cap and bathrobe. She left the bedroom and in a few seconds I heard the shower running. When she came back into the bedroom, her skin was bright pink and the veins in her shining breasts were easy to see. I said, "RoyReena, you have got to let me out of this kennel. You could get yourself into a lot of serious trouble with the law. If you let me out now, I'll just forget the whole thing. I am not a dog, RoyReena."

But she didn't act as though she'd heard. I was an invisible man without the power of speech, locked in an invisible cage.

She put on her green dress, fixed her hair, put on some makeup, and left the trailer, all the while pretending that my steady stream of words was not getting past my lips. When I heard the door of the trailer slam shut and the lock click, I yelled a dirty name, meaning her.

If it's hard for you to believe that such things can actually happen, imagine how *I* felt. I had spent part of a night and a full day locked up like a mongrel! Now it looked like it was going to be another night, and then maybe another day. Maybe it would run into a week or even weeks! Months! The rest of my life! Well, I got scared then. Really scared. A man is not meant to live as a crazy woman's pet. Being scared like that got my guts to rumbling. I squatted over the bedpan and let fly. I cleaned myself up and then crawled over to the far end of the cage to get away from the stink. That's when I made a discovery that I hate to tell you about, for it just goes to prove how dumb a man can be. Over in the far end of the cage I saw carpet. The mat fell about a quarter inch short of covering the whole floor of the cage, and in that quarter-inch gap I saw green pile carpet, the same green pile carpet that covered the rest of the bedroom floor. I picked up the corner of the mat and looked at another patch of unobstructed green pile. It was exactly what I should have done when I first woke up caged, but for reasons you will have to judge for yourself, it never occurred to me to do that simple thing. What I discovered was this: that goddamned dog cage didn't have any floor to it! All I had to do to get out of it was lift it up. And that's what I did. I got into a squatting position and stood up until my back pressed against the ceiling of the cage. Then I kept on rising up, and the cage, which probably weighed no more than sixty or seventy pounds, rose up with me. I stood it on one end and just walked out through the totally floorless floor, easy as that. I guess RoyReena figured that Rudy Mepps was not a prize-winning thinker. She was right.

I found my clothes piled neatly on her closet floor, got dressed, then found the telephone and called a taxi. While I waited for the cab, I took another look at the cage, just to emphasize to myself the awful extent of my stupidity, just in case I ever got the notion into my head to study atomic engineering. The whole episode made me want to laugh out loud, which I did. I laughed so hard my knees got weak and they buckled and I fell down. Tears came into my eyes and my arms went limp as overcooked noodles. I laughed for ten minutes or more, until my eyes ached for the lack of tears and my throat pinched tight and soundless. Then I went into the bathroom and washed my face in cold water. Then I went back into the bedroom and cleaned up the mess I had made —my bedpan, the plate of food, the magazines, and the newspaper. I found a note pad and a pencil and left a note for RoyReena Mepps, who had probably gone to the movies with Marva Sloane, if there was a Marva Sloane.

Dear R.R.
That was no way to get your Rudy. Use your head, girl. A man in a cage isn't worth a dime. Thanks for your hospitality, though, and I don't mean that as a sour joke or anything. We'll just forget about the nutty part.
Your friend,
Ulysses C.

My cab came. The weasel-faced driver didn't look at me but only grunted like an animal of doubtful trustworthiness when I told him to find a motel close to the hospital, and we didn't exchange another word between us until we got there.

I rented a room with two double beds, ordered a meal from room service, watched TV until midnight, then fell into a stony sleep.

I woke up at nine-thirty the next morning, dressed, and walked over to the hospital, where young Dr. Peach-fuzz told me that Sadass was dead. Dead! "That's not possible" is what I said, as if that was the most improbable thing that could have happened among the long list of improbable things that already had.

"I don't understand it either," said the kid. "We didn't find a thing in the tests." He was nervous and shifty, as if he had made a big mistake but didn't have any idea of what it was. I was afraid he was going to start bawling. "I swear Mr. Haygood was healthy as an ox. Blood pressure of a high-school sprinter. Magnificent lungs. Heart of a bull. My personal opinion was that he was suffering from extreme fatigue. But fatigue isn't usually fatal."

I didn't believe it. It seemed damned unlikely that genies are afflicted with mortality like the rest of us are. But when they took me downstairs to a basement room they called the icebox, where they kept dead bodies until a mortuary got around to picking them up, I saw it was true. There he was, on a table covered with a white sheet, all seven and a half feet of him stone-cold to the world. I picked up the sheet off his face and it was death all right. Once you've seen it, you don't forget what it looks like. The eyes were open a slit and showed a milk-gray film, the lips were blue and stiff-looking, the cheeks were sunk in. Dead. Doornail-dead. Dr. Peach-fuzz left me alone with him, thinking that I needed a minute by myself, but I didn't shed a tear and only felt a little queasy and weak of knee.

I guess I stood there for five minutes or so before it happened. It was something that didn't exactly catch me unprepared, considering what I'd been through recently. The big dead head of the genie began to rise up off the table as if he had some invisible confederate standing behind him and lifting it up. The head moved like a dead weight on a bad hinge, and when it was nearly upright, it turned toward me. The mouth opened slowly and the dark tongue moved. I heard some dry clickings, and then his voice, hoarse and thick with the death rattle, wheezed out. His eyes were still fogged over and blind. He said, "Ulysses." If it had been another name, I wouldn't have been able to understand it.

"Is that you, Sadass?" I says, whispering.

"Uh-huh. I went and died on you, chief."

"I can see that. But you don't seem to be all the way dead."

"No. It's true, all right. I'm dead, dead as a stone."

"But you're talking to me." I felt a little giddy. It's not often you find yourself involved in an argument with a corpse.

"Listen. That visit to your wife flat did me in. You shouldn't put such a strain on me. I don't seem to be what I once was, way back when. Everything's changed. I need you to help me out of this bind, pardner."

"Help you out? You're dead. Why don't you ask me to change water into Vino Fino?"

"I know I'm dead. But it doesn't have to be permanent. And I'm not going to ask you to do anything a little kid of six couldn't do."

I felt a dribble of pee tickle my leg. My ruined kidneys weren't going to take much more of this. "What do you want me to do?" I said.

"They're going to take me to the Smythe-Jennings-Yarnell mortuary. I want you to go out and pick up some things for me. Then you have to get to the mortuary before they embalm me. That's important. I'll tell you what to do when you get there."

He named a bunch of things, most of which I had heard of, herbs, powders, juices, then asked me if I thought I could find them in Las Vegas stores. I told him I could get most of the stuff at health-food stores and the rest of it at a Safeway. Then he gave me instructions on what to do with the stuff after I got it. I'll give you some of the ingredients here and a hint or two of how I was supposed to prepare them, but I won't go into absolute detail lest someone who might get his hands on these pages gets it into his head to run around the country resurrecting the dead by way of having a lark at the expense of a lot of innocent people's peace of mind. It was basically a poultice, just like your grandma used to make. Henbane, red clover, a pinch of belladonna, some common teas, pulp of Aloe vera, all made into a plaster that used egg whites as a binder. Some turpentine, and the leaves from any vine plant such as ivy, but sweet potato leaves will do just as well, about two handfuls of them, a pint of blood from a freshly butchered ox (I was pretty sure there wouldn't be a freshly butchered ox available in Las Vegas, so I substituted on my own a pint of ordinary beef blood, which I got at the meat section of Safeway), beeswax, eucalyptus oil, the water in which an infant under the age of three months had been bathed (I had to convince a young mother in the suburbs that I was the loser in a bet with my cronies about the outcome of a lizard race, and this being a town of gamblers, she didn't think it was farfetched at all, and gave me a bucket full of pissy water), a quart of fig juice, and the letters A O Z M cut from the skin of a duck. I used a cab to do all my running around and then went back to the motel room to do my mixing and preparing. I'd bought a half dozen plastic pails at Safeway for the job. When I had the poultice ready, I filled a pail and called a cab.

The Smythe-Jennings-Yarnell funeral home was one of those posh-looking places on the edge of an old residential district, sort of like an Old South plantation house, with big white columns and doors tall enough to let in giraffes. I told the receptionist that I was Tyrone Haygood's dad and that I wanted to "view the remains privately." She called for Mr. Yarnell over her intercom and in about half a minute he came out of an office that glowed cherry-red inside due to the plush carpet and rosy wallpaper.

Yarnell was a white-faced waxy man who wore a narrow band of blue-black hair sideways across his head from ear to ear, without benefit of a part. He had a little rosebud mouth with Cupid lips cut in an undying smile. His nose was long and narrow and his eyes seemed wet. He was wearing an eggshell-yellow blazer, green slacks, a brown shirt with a white tie, and a pair of those spectator shoes that were sharp enough to kick a hole through a dime. He was slicker than a snake's toenails.

"Ah, my dear man" is what he said as he took hold of my hand in his. It felt like the hand of a cold child. I noticed his eyes flicking, quick as a frog's tongue, down toward my bucket full of stinking goo, but he didn't ask me about it. "We have something very *very* nice in the mid-price range." He led me into a room full of caskets.

"I just want to see my boy," I said.

"You'll find that we take great pride in our product, Mr. Haygood. In times of personal loss, the primary consideration must always be—"

"Just take me to see my boy, Mr. Yarnell," I said.

"Of course, of course. There will be time later to make the

arrangements. I think you will soon see that our product here at Smythe-Jennings-Yarnell is second to none."

He stood there smiling, waiting for me to show him how impressed I was, but I just let him wait. Then he said, "Ah-ha," as if the light had finally dawned on him, and he led me out toward the back of the funeral parlor, where there was a flight of stairs that went down steep into darkness. At the bottom of the stairs, there was a heavy door. Yarnell unlocked it and hefted it open.

It was a bright room made out of white tile and about as big as a hotel lobby. There were about a dozen stiffs lying on tables under sheets. But I didn't have any trouble picking out Sadass, who outsized his fellow recently departed by double. I walked over to him.

"Has he been embalmed yet?" I asked.

Yarnell stuttered. "Why, no. Mr. St. Martin won't be here until two. It's his day to play baccarat. They take turns, our employees I mean, and—"

"I don't want to hear about it," I said, peevish, and only half pretending.

"Ah." But he just stood there shaking hands with himself.

"See you later, Mr. Yarnell," I said.

He looked mixed up. He gave my bucket another quick look, but let his eyes stop on it long enough to let me know that he was curious and would I like to explain.

"Look, Yarnell," I said. "I got my eyes on that slick black coffin with the gold scrollwork on the sides, the one with the red, white, and blue satin upholstery—must cost a couple of thousand dollars at least—but unless you give me ten minutes alone with Tyrone here, I swear I'll bury him myself in a packing crate."

Yarnell adjusted his tie until he winced, but then backed

out of the room, bowing from the neck and smiling like a headwaiter who'd been slipped a twenty. He said "Ah" one more time before he ducked through the door, which he closed carefully, as if an accidental slam would have the stiffs jumping off the tables.

I waited a minute, then yanked the sheet off Sadass. He looked worse than before. The blue-white tinge under his brown skin made me shiver. His chest was sunk in and his lips had drawn back off his mossy teeth, which made him appear to be straining at stool. I didn't linger on his appearance, though. Instead, I picked up the bucket and began smearing the poultice all over him. It had gotten a little stiff, and the going was hard. I was afraid there wouldn't be enough of it, as it was going on so thick, but I did manage to get him all covered over with it, leaving only two or three bare spots. When I got to his face, I stuck the small plastic funnel (which I had gotten at Safeway) into his mouth and then formed a seal around it with the plaster. While it got hard, I toured the room and found what I needed next: a sink. It was a big sink with four faucets. Two of the faucets had rubber hoses attached to them. I got the pail and washed it out carefully. Then I filled it with about an inch of lukewarm water.

The next step was the hardest one of all, and I needed a minute to prepare myself for it. I was a little afraid that Yarnell or one of his employees might walk in, and I tried to think up something to say to them, just in case, such as, "My son and me belong to an unusual religious sect headquartered in Tibet, and this here is part of the burial rites that we customarily use. You're not going to deny a man the right to practice his religion-of-choice, are you, Mr. Yarnell?" But no one came in.

The steak knife was also from Safeway. I held it against my finger for a second. What in blazes am I doing this for? I asked myself. It was a good question. I didn't answer it. Instead, I drew the serrated edge across the meaty part of the middle finger of my left hand and let it bleed for a minute into the bucket. Blood. The sight of it always made me light-headed. But I stayed on my feet and let the finger drip. Then I slapped on a Safeway Band-Aid.

I went back to Sadass and raised the bucket with its slightly pink water to the funnel. Then I let it loose, into the funnel, slowly. It burbled home.

Nothing happened. He didn't twitch. My finger ached. Then I heard footsteps coming down the stairs. Quick as a rat, I yanked the funnel out of Sadass's mouth, tossed it into the bucket, and pulled the sheet over his body. I dropped to my knees. I heard the door open carefully behind me and felt the rush of warm air from the stairwell on my back.

I started mumbling prayers: "O Lord of our fathers and of our fathers' fathers, O eternal light, O many-eyed all-seeing thousand-footed fire-winged presence who cometh in the bleakest night—" (Not being a religious man, I had to improvise on the spot, using the first holy-sounding words that popped into my head, but I kept it in a low mumble so that Yarnell couldn't be sure of exactly what he heard and then call me down for a fake) "—O stomper of sinning malcontents and creepers, O hater of the wino's shit-breath lies, Lord of the fiery eyes of retribution, have mercy upon this here lowlife doer of contemptible tricks, this great farting heathen reprobate Turk or whatever the hell he is, whom the angels spitteth upon venomously—" (I felt I was on safe ground now because I didn't feel the warm air on my back any more, which meant that Yarnell must have seen me on my knees praying for my boy and didn't want to risk blowing the sale of the fanciest coffin he had in stock by interrupting a grieving father in the middle of his goodbye, but I went on with it anyway, just to be sure) "—mercy mercy, Lord, on these sots, bums, dopes, snakes, sneaks, snipes, hogs, thieves, brutes, kooks, turds, slobs, jerks, punks, rats, thugs, hicks, hammer the light of glory into their dead eyes and unclog their heads once and for all, or else drop the whole miserable show right now in its bloody tracks, we've got nothing to lose, the way I see it, since we keep losing everything we've got anyway, year after year, time after time, loss, loss, after loss—"

"Hold on, chief," says Sadass from under the sheet. "You're running off at the mouth in a careless way. Don't get the foolish notion that words spoken out loud don't mean anything."

"Sadass! Is that you?"

"It ain't the Mayor of Mexicali, effendi."

He swung his legs off the table, wriggled his toes for a second, then tested his legs on the solid floor, like a sailor who's been at sea for a year. He was a little wobbly. He peeled the plaster off his face. It came off easy. I won't say he looked good as new, but he sure was not a dead Efrite any more.

"Listen, chief," he says. "We have got to get our signals straightened out. There's a limit to what I can do these days. I don't like it, but I guess it's something we are going to have to live with, like it or not." He was stripping the gunk off his body and piling it in a neat little pyramid.

I didn't like his tone. "Listen yourself, you big ape. I never told you to take me on that plane trip into the hereafter. If you had asked, maybe all this wouldn't have happened. What good did it do me, anyway? Finding out all that bushwah about this so-called Ansel Roe, which I still don't believe. You think you did me a favor?"

"The thing is, boss," he says, stripping the last bit of that plaster off his feet, "I can't afford to spend so much energy in one lump sum. You won't believe this, but back in the old days I could ferry a whole barge full of potentates around the universe to converse with the angels themselves, devils too, and the obscure gods that rule our lives, you name it, keeping them ass-deep in fried chicken all the while, and I always felt in the pink afterwards. The way the world is now, you're lucky I could even manage to tell you how to bring me back from the Underworld in one piece."

"Real lucky," I says, not intending for it to sound as sour as it did.

But he ignored the crack. "See, the world, the whole universe, I mean *this* universe, the one you people live in, is like—"

"I know," I says. "A rotten peach."

"Right! This entropy, like they say, has flattened out nearly every last pocket of energy, even my kind of energy, which is of a special kind. I'm not sure what's going to happen here, but I flat don't like the smell of it, chief. I would say, though, that time is not on your side."

Well, an unfortunate thing happened. As we gabbed, Mr. Yarnell walked in. I didn't hear him over the noise of our talking, and of course, he was a man who didn't make any noise at all—I figured even his farts whispered—and so I didn't get a chance to invent a story that would set his mind at ease. Not that it mattered much, for I don't know what I could have said to him that would have made him believe that Tyrone Haygood's return to the world of the living was nothing to get worked up about.

Yarnell made a giant squeak, like a one-hundred-pound mouse confronting a one-thousand-pound cat, and both Sadass and I turned to look at him. "This is Mr. Yarnell," I says to Sadass, meaning to be sociable.

*Eight will be* shorter than the rest. This is 8, just the same. I had to tear out a bunch of pages. Over half, I guess.

Maybe I do chase it too much. The grape, I mean. But I get depressed sometimes. I get lonely. I get to counting my regrets. You think back on what you could have done with your life if you hadn't been so dumb or timid. You think, I could have gone this way instead of that. But at the time it doesn't seem so clear-cut. At the time, there is only one reasonable way to do a thing. Then you look back on it and see that you had blinders on. Who put them there? You did. Who else. You are dumb. Face it like a man. Dumb. Everyone is Einstein when it comes to hindsight. But in the thick of the fray you're dumb.

I get the chilblains just lying in bed, warm and dry. Old age.

Sometimes I wish I had Sadass back here with me. Sometimes I think I know exactly what I'd do with him and how I'd fix my life. But it's wrong. I did the right thing. Here I am, here I stay, I'll see it through to the end. Holloway will see to it that I get buried next to Emily, some of the oldsters will stand by my grave with their gray heads bowed while some hired preacher says what he's paid to say, maybe Vi will be there too, her king-size jars leaning over the fresh-turned earth.

Dry rot of the brain. Like the trunk of an old tree. I had some old trees on my land. I felt pity for them. I'd talk to them, congratulating them for the good work they'd done over the years, keeping them as comfortable as I could during the cold season, dumping fresh loads of red earthworms into their roots, for they love that, and the fruit they bear in the last years of their lives is the sweetest.

Dry rot of the brain. Senility. I'm not so scared of it as I was. There's a sweetness that comes with it. A calm. Sometimes I feel like a water bird floating in a pond. Is that senile? I don't know. All I know is that I don't feel scared. Lonely, depressed, sometimes, but not scared. So I chase the grape.

They don't care. The staff, I mean. The others sometimes gossip or stare, for there are some teetotalers and busybodies here.

I tore out over half the pages of this eighth notebook because of what I had filled them with. It was a lot of excuse-making and justifying. It was a lot of arguing. I was doing a lot of drinking. See the stains? It isn't purple ink. That up there in the corner is a fleck of puke. I mean, I went after it hard. Lost most of a week. I started to see things I knew weren't there.

I saw Emily. She sat in a chair and talked to me. She was about thirty years old. She arranged flowers and talked about the beautiful new department store going up in the Camino Valley east of San Soledad. I called her on it, but she didn't answer me. She wasn't there. Dry rot of the brain.

Ansel Roe came. We had a fight. You've seen winos boxing the air? A pathetic sight. Drop by any Main Street bar, any time of day. There he'll be, sitting at the bar mumbling to himself, or in a booth holding on to his head, and suddenly he jumps up and screams something obscene into the face of an invisible visitor. He'll throw a wino punch. You've seen those? Moves about one inch per minute and couldn't do harm to a cobweb. So I had it out with a mirage. Vi came in and led me back to bed. I tried to hit her, but she just picked me up and tucked me in and said some soothing words into my stinking face. She's a nice girl.

Holloway came in and told a joke about a man who had to drink tea through his asshole. I didn't get it, but then I couldn't understand much of anything during this time. I would watch TV, but one program would run into another and I would have a fit because the killer in one program was tap-dancing in another. It was different programs, different actors, but to me it was all one tangled play, channel to channel, hour to hour.

Dry rot of the brain.

Happens to everybody, sooner or later.

Anyway, I came out of it. I tapered off. I didn't make a big decision about it or try to pull myself together, I just passed out for a day and a half, and when I woke up I was hungry and I went down to the cafeteria and had me a big lunch and then I went out for a walk along the beach feeling a need for the fresh ocean breeze, and that was it. It was over. I felt better for it, too. No regrets.

I went back to my room and looked at notebook number 8. Well, it was a mess. Even my handwriting—which isn't very good to begin with—looked like the hand of a backward child. Big shaky scrawl. Every sentence ended with a big black exclamation mark. I had drawn some stupid pictures. Knives dripping blood. A heart broke in two. The face of a cat. A hand holding a pistol. Lips. Eyes. Tits (Vi's). Bottles. A tin lamp. Smoke in the shape of a man. Sadass.

I tore those pages out and threw them away. They would only waste your time. What do you care about a wine-drinking spree and the pipe dreams and mirages of an old sot? Nothing.

In the beginning I said I was not a wino. I hold to that. That spree was a first for me. And my last. But believe what you want.

Let's get back to the real story. If you've made it this far, it wasn't because you had a burning interest in my bad habits or my temporary lapses into stupidity.

So let 8 start fresh here.

## 8

"This is Mr. Yarnell," I says to Sadass, meaning to be sociable.

Yarnell. I wish I could draw. For I would like to draw you a picture of his face.

His wet eyes got big as quarters. His jaw moved up and down. He started in making muh-muh-muh sounds, after that first big squeak. He was white. He was pasty to begin with, but now he was pastier. Like dough.

I'll say this for him, though: he must have had some solid training in good manners when he was a young child. For they came to his rescue now. He said, "Pleased to make your acquaintance, sir," and he didn't even stutter. You might think that a man faced with a similar situation would do something nutty—scream, run, faint, or pray. Not Yarnell. He sticks out his pale hand and offers to shake with Sadass, the naked resurrected giant Efrite. Enough can't be said for early training.

"Where's my duds, Yarnell?" says Sadass.

Yarnell's face split open in a white smile, but he looked

about as happy as a hypochondriac in a leper colony. "Ah, unfortunately, sir, we have already disposed of them."

"Is that so?" says Sadass, still holding on to the funeral director's hand. "First you try to put a man into the ground, and then you tell him you've thrown away his clothes. This your idea of a joke, Yarnell?"

Sadass was laying it on a little bit too thick. "Seems like the joke is on Yarnell," I says.

Yarnell's eyes began to shift back and forth between me and Sadass, as if he's just beginning to add 2 and 2. He licked his Kewpie-doll lips, his little tongue darting in and out, and he says, "This is Clint's doing, isn't it?"

By way of reply, Sadass cuts a fart. The accumulated gas of a man twelve hours dead isn't one of the sweeter aromas to be found in nature.

"Clint Jennings, am I right?" says Yarnell, beginning to show some color in his face. "He made a bet with Bobby Smythe that he could make me soil my Sans-a-belts." Yarnell slapped his thigh. "Well, he loses! Oh, sure, you gave me a moment's fright, Mr. Haygood, you surely did. *But I did not soil my Sans-a-belts!*"

We had a good laugh, Yarnell and me. Yarnell wiped his eyes. I was laughing just to be sociable, but Yarnell was gripped by the humor of it all. His laugh, though, was just about as noiseless as everything else about him, sort of a paralyzation of his lungs and throat, while his helpless jaws fell open and his lips drew back off his teeth like there was a winch at the back of his head that was reeling in the skin of his face, making his eyes pop too. His knees buckled and he leaned on Sadass's table for support. He was shaking his head in a disbelieving way, overwhelmed at the extremes some people will go to just to carry off a practical joke. When he could talk again, he said, "Oh boy oh boy, that Clint Jennings is a card, isn't he?" Then he buckled over again, gripped by another hard onslaught of silent laughing. One thing you can say for this undertaker, he appreciated a sense of humor. "Ye gods!" he says, laying across the table from the waist up. "What was the bet, anyway? A hundred? Five? A thousand?" He patted the back of his pants weakly. "Clean!" he said, half screaming. "Clean as a whistle!"

Sadass all the while is looking at Yarnell with a sour expression on his face. "I don't like this so-called man," he says to me.

"He's just an undertaker," I says, as if that explained something.

"I know what he *is*," says Sadass, sounding peeved. "It doesn't matter to me what in the hell he is, I just don't like him. He could be a goddamned piano tuner and he'd still turn my stomach."

I would have thought that Efrites were above such petty irritations. But what did I know? What do I know now, to this day? Nothing.

"Let's go," I says.

"How am I supposed to do that?" asks Sadass, acting kind of hot, even toward me now. I guess he forgot that I was the one responsible for bringing him back to life. Come to think of it, I don't recall that Lazarus had much to say by way of thanks after climbing out of his hole. Well, ingratitude is not one of the more unique human qualities. "This so-called man here has taken my clothes and dumped them," says Sadass.

I looked at him. What a dummy. "Make yourself a nice suit then," I says. "Snap your fingers, clap your hands, do what you do."

He shook his head. "It's the principle of it."

"Then wrap that sheet around you and let's get our rear ends out of here."

"Shit!" is what he says. He was hot.

"Cut it out, Sadass," I says. I could see that he was getting himself into a sulk.

Yarnell had recovered from his fit of laughing. He was wiping his eyes with a handkerchief. Silk. Rose color. I grabbed Sadass by the arm and pulled him toward the door. He came along with me but then stopped short. "Wait up," he says. He looked back at Yarnell, who was now straightening his tie and smoothing his yellow lapels.

Sadass made a gesture in the air. I thought it was meant to be obscene, but it's too elaborate for that. It was hocus-pocus stuff, for it made things happen.

The stiffs, about a dozen of them, sat straight up. Their sheets fell away from them. Their muscles were quivering with some kind of nervous electricity. Their skin was a yellowy green and slightly transparent. Their eyes were wide-open like they were shocked awake, but they were also milky and blind-looking. Their mouths had a rigor-mortis twist to them so that they all showed their gray teeth in a terrible way, like they were smiling, snarling, and wincing at the same time.

My mouth went dry in a second. My heart stopped, then took off like a sparrow. My first notion was to get through that doorway out of there, but Sadass grabbed my arm before I moved a step.

"Wait a minute," he says.

Yarnell didn't notice the rising up of his dead clientele, for his back was turned to the rows of tables.

"Okay," says Sadass. "That's it. Let's go."

"Go?" I yanked his arm. "You can't just do something mean like that and go! You can't—" But my powers of speech were robbed by the scene that was developing before my eyes. The corpses had all slid off their tables and were now walking, hands outstretched in the sleepwalker's way, toward Yarnell, who still had his eggshell-yellow back turned to them. The stiffs were moving slow, scuffing their dead feet on the tile floor, raising a dry hissing sound that no one in his right mind would ever want to listen to for very long.

"Come on," says Sadass. "I want to get something to eat right away. The only way I'm going to keep ahead of this entropy business is to keep stoked up on food. Otherwise, I am going to drop over on you again. This is serious, chief."

The stiffs were about a yard away from Yarnell, and Sadass wanted to go out for a bite to eat. They were not moving very fast, and he could have run away from them if he understood his danger, but he just stood there. It was like one of those old-time B-movies. The stiffs were moving on him with hands outstretched, like zombies out to get revenge on the fiend who had tried to use them for his unwholesome purposes. Everyone in the audience can see it coming and they wonder why the fiend can't. Some fool who always takes movies seriously will yell out a warning.

That's what I did. I couldn't help myself. I says, "Yarnell! Duck!" and pointed at the crowd of stiffs coming up behind him.

Yarnell was still grinning and wiping tears away from his eyes. "Ah-ha-ha," he said in a genteel laugh, able to control himself now against the crazy sense of humor of his partner.

"Look out!" I hollered, for the outstretched dead fingers were only inches from his throat now.

He finally turned. He squeaked again. Louder this time. He filled his Sans-a-belt slacks. He buckled over. He dropped to his hands and knees and lowered himself slowly toward the floor like a man searching for a small diamond that had just popped out of his tie clip.

All together, just as if they had been rehearsing it this way, the stiffs dropped their arms and widened their grins. It was an awful sight. Yarnell looked like a man in a nightmare, trying to get traction on all fours, but stuck in the sand. He was too weak to get anywhere. The stiffs were standing around him, and Yarnell was trying to swim away between their legs. He was screaming. It was a quiet scream that you almost couldn't hear, for even his lungs were sapped by fear.

"Sadass!" I says. "You can't do this! This poor undertaker can't take it! Think of his wife and kids. Think of—"

"To hell with the miserable little prick," says Sadass, in an unnecessarily hotheaded way. I figured he was a little off his rocker from being dead all that time. Why else was he taking it out on this poor Yarnell, who was only doing his job? "I don't give a shit about him or his family!" he roars into my face. "Let him squirm in hell, the little cheese-eating pecker-head!"

You'd think that this Yarnell was the mastermind of a ring of child-torturers, the way Sadass was carrying on.

The grinning stiffs all backed away from the swimming undertaker. They paired off, the men with the women—there were six men and four women and two men had to pair off with each other but they were a long way from worrying about how it might look—and they began to dance, a stiff-legged waltz in death-time, to a slow funeral-procession drum. You could almost hear it, like a big stone heart rumbling under the tile floor—*boom boom boom*—as the stiffs clomped around that room, the strangest ballroom dance human eyes had ever seen or would want to.

Yarnell lost all ability to swim. He collapsed and rolled over onto his side. He was still conscious, but he had a distant look in his eyes and he was sort of crooning sweetly to himself and making big spit bubbles. He had messed his slacks more than once. He looked like a child in a crib playing with its hands. His hands were spiders, then they were birds, now they were little boats. He said, "Nu-nu, mi-mi, mummy, gump."

We left him like that. The stiffs climbed back onto their tables, but Yarnell wasn't ever going to be the same again. We climbed the stairs, crossed through the showroom of caskets, and went out the front doors of the mortuary. I didn't even look at the receptionist. Sadass was wrapped up in his sheet, refusing, out of spite, to create himself a set of clothes.

"I shouldn't have done that," says Sadass, acting a little saner. It was nice to be out in the sunlight again, where everything had hard edges and was easy to understand.

"You're telling me," I says. "Why didn't you just slit his throat if he bothered you that much?"

"The hell with Yarnell. No, I meant I shouldn't have used up energy like that, especially after just coming back to life myself. The treatment you gave me was only an emergency boost, and not meant to give me back full power."

I couldn't believe my ears. I got hot. "You dope! You did a lot of damage to an innocent man who was just doing his job!"

Sadass gives me a sly look. "Innocent?"

"You know what I mean."

"I do, but do you?"

We stood there looking at each other for a few seconds. The air between us could have been filled with cement.

Then he throws his arm around my shoulder in a friendly way, rubbing out any disagreement that might have been trying to come between us. "Aw, Yarnell will be all right," he says. "By tomorrow he'll be believing it was all a bad dream. He'll swear off, start going to church regularly, and treat his kids better."

"You sure?"

"Why would I lie to you?"

"I don't know."

"And you're the boss, aren't you? What you say goes, right?"

"That's right," I says, but I wasn't sure about that at all. Not at all.

We took a cab back to the motel room I had rented, and then I called an Italian restaurant that delivered full meals by truck. I ordered about forty dollars' worth of spaghetti, meatballs, pizza, and lasagna. It took about an hour for it to arrive. I paid the kid with a crisp fifty that Sadass had plucked from the air.

Sadass didn't look too perky. I was afraid he was going to die again. But after he had eaten about ten plates full of food he was his old grinning self.

"The way I've got it figured," he says, "I'll have to eat about every four or five hours, or else I'll be putting out more energy than I'll be able to generate."

I had a little wine and a plate of spaghetti. It was good spaghetti. I felt better. I had a question for Sadass. It was a dumb question, but I asked it anyway.

"How can you turn food into magical powers?"

He had a mouthful of lasagna. "Easy," he said, spitting cheese. "Matter and energy are the same thing. Everything you can lay your eyes on is the same thing. Invisible stuff is the same thing as visible stuff. There is only one trick in the deck."

"What's that?"

"Form."

"Form?"

"Form. The power to give shape is the only power there is."

"Oh," I said.

He bent down to his food and began to eat seriously. I guess he figured he'd answered my question.

That's it. I told you this would be a short one.

*Nine.* It's all here, no missing pages. I've eased back on the drinking. I feel better. You've been drunk. So you know the feeling of high-minded floating that comes after a binge. After the hangover. A kind of cottony feeling. The world still presses on you, but you are insulated. That makes you friendlier. You can talk to people you'd not ordinarily give the time of day to. Your thoughts are philosophical. You're still a little drunk, that's all.

We sat in that motel for a long while not doing much at all. Sadass just wanted to rest up and digest his food. We watched TV. I went out for some newspapers and magazines. From a phone booth I called the Smythe-Jennings-Yarnell funeral home.

"How's Mr. Yarnell feeling?" I asked the receptionist.

"They haven't called yet," she said.

I gave that some thought. "The doctors?"

"The hospital."

"Is he, well, *sick*?"

"They're calling it a virus."

"He'll be glad to hear that," I said.

She said, "What?"

"Some viruses can get to the brain. Fever. That's just what he's going to want to hear."

"I'm afraid I don't understand."

"That's all right. You don't need to. Goodbye."

I walked back to the motel. Sadass was in bed, propped up on the pillows, watching a soap opera.

I took a bath to wash off what I figured to be a death-room stink.

Laying in the hot water, I had time to think things over. But my mind was narrow. I guess a better person than me would have been inclined to get philosophical about the nature of the world, having spent as much time as I had with a real genie. Not me. I kept coming back to Ansel Roe. There was a knot of anger in the middle of my brain. It was tight, and I was picking away at it with brittle fingernails.

Ansel Roe. I didn't want to believe he was real, but that knot in my brain was as real as anything I'd ever felt.

I told myself: That all happened a long time ago. But the mind will dwell on the worst, no matter how remote it is.

A man is a perverse thing in nature.

I read a book once a long time ago about a man who felt justified about everything he did, no matter how low-down it was. He died cursing the blue sky. He was miserable. I don't know why I read the damn book. I guess I wanted to see how he was going to get out of the mess he had made for himself. He didn't. Everything went from bad to worse. But to listen to him whine, it was everybody's fault but his own. He took up a hermit's life, but he was still miserable. But as a hermit, he had no one to carp at except the trees and stones. "You goddamned tree," he would say. "Rock, you son of a bitch." Like that. Then he got sick and died. He was laying on his back in a field of weeds. "F—— you, sky" was the last thing he said. Pardon my French, but I just wanted to let you know what his last words were. He was a stupid man.

I guess I am stupid too. Not as bad off as he was, but surely no Einstein either. So I dwelt on Ansel Roe, when I should have been dwelling on miracles.

Here is how a man can be a perverse thing: no matter how good a woman is to him, just let some yahoo come along and suggest that she has been unfaithful, the fool husband will eventually wind up believing the worst. It will eat on him, for no man is secure enough in the knowledge of his own worth to be completely insulated from such lying gossip. A man will doubt himself with relish if he is offered the chance, no matter how rewarding his life has been up to that point.

A perverse thing. If you tell a hairy man that he is a closer relative to the jungle apes than a smooth man, he will start shaving his face all the way down to his collarbones and take to wearing starched shirts. He knows he is a man and not an ape, but a little spark of doubt has been fanned up into a flame by a stupid remark.

I thought about RoyReena Mepps just to get that Ansel Roe out of my mind. I liked her a lot, in spite of her craziness. I wished she wasn't going to be unhappy for the rest of her life. She was basically a good girl and didn't deserve to be the victim of her crackpot notions. Like I said, people will victimize themselves. It's perverse. It's a tiresome thought.

I left the tub feeling somewhat blue, so I started to watch a game show on the TV to get my mind on simpler things. But Sadass, who's been dozing, cuts in with a big musical yawn and sits up. "I'm feeling my olden-days self again," he croons. "But now hear this, chief: we have got to stay on our toes from here on out. One thing at a time. Go slow. Our motto should be, Safety First. Let's start using our heads, okay?"

I just gave him the sour look he deserved. I wasn't about to remind him again, though, that I had never asked him to do a damned thing for me. Not directly, at least.

Then, like in the comic strips, a light bulb gets turned on over my head. An idea. "There's this woman I'd like you to do something for," I says. "If and when you feel up to it."

He gives me a sly sideways look. "Why, you old dog," he says, between his grinning teeth.

I ignored the dumb crack. "She's a little crazy from being alone all her life. What she needs is a real man, not a dream of one. Can you fix her up?"

"You mean you want me to strip some years off of you, so that you can fill the bill?"

"No. Not me. You don't need to do a damned thing for me. I want you to give her somebody called Rudy Mepps. He ran off twenty-two years ago because they had a spat. Now I want him to come home, with his hat in his hand."

"Where is he now?"

"He isn't anywhere. She made him up out of her head. I told you she was a little crazy. But I want you to take that made-up dream story of hers and make it into a real one in her own mind, which it already nearly is, right down to the last detail. That shouldn't be too hard for someone who can make a corpse dance, should it? Then—now this might be a little more than you can handle—I want you to invent this Rudy Mepps character in the flesh." I told him the whole story of Mepps more or less the way RoyReena told it to me and described him right down to his natty fingernails. "But now he's older, about sixty-five, and he looks something like me. Healthier, though. He's got to have a good pump, somewhat burly, and his plumbing has to be in good working order—if you get what I mean."

Sadass rolled his big head sideways again and gives me a raised-eyebrow look. But I ignored it.

"This afternoon I want Rudy Mepps to stroll into Porky's Chop House—that place you passed out in front of yesterday. I want her to recognize him and I want him to recognize her. Then I want him to beg for forgiveness and ask her if he can come back home. He should have a bouquet of flowers in his hand. Roses. I want her to say yes. I want them to have a nice little honeymoon that night and then live happily ever after. Except for one hitch."

"Hitch?"

"Well, I want him to treat her like the Queen of Ethiopia. He needs to think she's the most highly-thought-of good-looking woman in this town. Make him a little jealous. This is what a woman like RoyReena needs to pump up her self-confidence and shed her insane ways."

Sadass gave out a big sigh. "You're a thoughtful man, Ulysses Cinder," he says.

"Thoughts are all I've got."

He rubbed at his eyes, said it was done, then he ate a whole loaf of garlic bread, and after washing it down with a cup of coffee, he took a nap.

I went out for a walk. I felt pretty good about myself. Picture how good Andrew Carnegie felt after shelling out a few million to give some town in the Middle West its own opera house. That's how I felt.

What happened to my high-minded notion that no one should tamper with the proper order of things? I forgot it.

Was I playing God? Did I think I had a new career? Ulysses Cinder, *God*? No. RoyReena Mepps was in a bad way. I helped her out. That's all. I didn't have any impulse to start regulating the rains or dispensing justice to sinners.

When I got back to the motel, Sadass was awake and pacing the floor.

"Something's happening," he says.

I looked around. Nothing was happening. "What?" I says.

He stopped pacing and looked at me. It was a big-eyed look. He almost looked afraid. "I'm going to die, Ulysses," he says.

"Not *again*," I says.

"I'm afraid so, effendi. But this time it's going to be permanent. I'm the last of the Efrites, and it looks like our time is over."

"Over?"

"Well, for now, anyway. The world is built on a seesaw principle. We are about to bump our butts on the playground."

"I don't get it."

"You don't have to. What do you know about the stars, Ulysses?"

"Not much. There's a lot of them, they're big, they're hot."

"And they die. And when they die they sometimes blow up first, giving off thousands of times as much light and heat as they ever did. It's called a nova."

"And then they go out?"

"Like a candle."

"What's that got to do with you?" I ask.

But instead of answering, he gives out a big yell, "Ya-eeee!" like that, like a nut, in a high-pitched voice that hurts my ears. Then he starts pacing back and forth again, wringing his hands, the floor bouncing, the furniture rattling.

"You going to explain, or are you just going to goose-step around this room?"

He sat down on the edge of the bed and held his head in his hands. I think he was blubbering. I thought: My genie has gone berserk.

He stopped blubbering. He started giggling. It went on

and on. So I sat down and opened a magazine. I figured he'd get on with his explanation when his fit passed.

I thumbed through the slick pages. There was an article about life in New Zealand, how good it was and how it was getting even better, as opposed to nearly everywhere else. There was something about the oil shortage. Someone had something to say about the absence of wild game in the supposed wilderness areas. Pictures of suntanned girls in skimpy bathing suits, smiling. Their teeth were perfect. Pictures of planets and stars taken from spaceships. A story about collapsed stars that were so heavy they swallowed their own light. A full-color picture of a firing squad in South America aiming their guns at a dwarfish-looking man who was tied to a post. It was all the usual stuff, but I thumbed through it twice, then I picked up another magazine with more pictures in it.

"Look," says Sadass.

I looked up from a picture of a naked lunatic attempting to fly. He was in the air, having just jumped off a ten-story building, his skinny arms out like wings.

"What am I supposed to be looking at?" I says.

"Me!" He stood up tall and flexed his arms. He looked better than ever. Better, bigger, stronger. "Something's happening."

"That's what you already said," I says.

"I sort of understand it too," he says, as if talking to a third party. "Like a star about to turn itself off, I'm blazing up to a thousand times more than I ever was."

"Ever?"

"Ever. Right now, if you wanted me to do it, I could turn the whole world into an old man's daydream."

It sounded like brag, but I didn't believe that it was. He

looked all-powerful. Even his eyes seemed to glow with an interior fire.

And then suddenly he was a bird. All at once I'm looking at a big ugly bird. Right there in front of me where Sadass had been standing, a big ugly bald-headed bird. A vulture. The vulture hops up on the bed and spreads its giant wings. My heart stopped dead, misfired, then took off. It wasn't fear or surprise, for what did I have to fear or be surprised at after all that had happened, but it was more like excitement, some kind of old memory in me was triggered, old desire kindled, but I didn't know what it was, though I longed for it.

"See how easy that was?" It was Sadass again, back to normal.

I nodded. But before my head could go all the way from down to up, I was looking at that bird again, only this time I was seeing it eye-to-eye, for now he had turned me into a vulture too.

"Sadass," I says, but my voice wasn't exactly my voice. It was kind of a snakelike hissing, but I knew what I was saying, and so did Sadass. "Don't go doing things for me any more, will you? I didn't say anything about wanting to be a goddamned bird."

"Wait up, little buddy," he says, hissing in my face. "We are going to have some great fun!"

"I don't want to be any damned bald-headed garbage-eating buzzard for any reason you or anyone else can think of, now or ever!" But even while I was hissing that message to him, I felt a deep and severe itch that I needed to satisfy bad. It was a good feeling. It got me excited as a child on Christmas morning. My bird heart was firing like a machine gun. Then I was me myself again, wingless and shaking and weak in the knees, and Sadass was himself too, and we were looking at each other in a motel room in Las Vegas, featherless, and I didn't know or care *why*, but one thing was for sure: for a split second there I felt a ferocious, high-order itch that would have felt ungodly good in satisfying.

"What did you do that for?" I ask, but I had a hunch about that.

"Because it was easy. Everything is going to be easy from here on out. The only thing is, time is getting short."

I got mad. "You pull tricks like that just because they are easy? What kind of dumb lamebrain thing is that to do?"

He held up his hand. "Not just for that alone, Ulysses," he says. "It occurs to me that humans suffer from a peculiar problem. On the one hand they know that they aren't really happy about much in their lives, and on the other hand they don't have very many good ideas about what being happy means."

Him saying that reminded me of RoyReena Mepps. I wondered if I had done the right thing in making her dreams come true. Maybe a real Rudy would throw her into despair, human beings being what they are. I said, "That's not exactly a news bulletin, Sadass."

"True. But I've got some ideas along those lines, ideas I've come up with after a long time of being used by humans who thought they knew exactly what they needed to make themselves happy, and since you've been smart enough to steer clear of those boomerangs—money, power, eternal youth, and all that bunkum—I thought you'd maybe like to try on my idea for size, to find out what it really means to be purely happy."

I only shrugged, but that was enough for this genie, who had a special knack for taking things for granted. We were vultures again, big heavy birds with black glossy feathers, hissing at each other like snakes, pink heads bald as stone.

We waddled around the room, testing our new feet, but

vultures just don't naturally walk too good. I said, "I don't get it. I thought that entropy business was making you weaker and weaker. Now you tell me about stars blowing up and dying." I lifted my wings, flexing out the long feathers on the tips. They felt like fingers, only more delicate, the fingers of a concert piano player.

"I know what you're thinking about," he says. "Those cops, the trouble I had getting them back to normal. Ulysses, I was at a low ebb then. Now that's gone. I've shot back up to the top, and to beyond the top. I'll come back down, pretty soon, and when I do, I'll have less power than a dead goldfish." He jumped past me and lit by the door. "Goddamn! You feel that itch, Ulysses?"

"What itch?" I knew exactly what he meant.

"To fly, dammit! Don't you feel it? It's got me half bawling with the need for it! If a vulture can bawl. I need to get into the air!"

So did I. That motel room was making me sick. Sadass opened the door with his beak and we waddled outside. A maid pushing a rolling hamper saw us. She stopped pushing. Her round pink face got long and white. She turned around very slowly and very slowly she walked away from us.

Sadass stretched out his wings and kicked up off the ground. He started to glide across the parking lot. He was big. Ten-foot wingspread at least. A black shape in the air glistening with power. He sailed over some cars, circled, came back to where I was standing. "What are you waiting for?" he says. "Let's get going!"

Well, it was funny. My wings felt like arms, except that they were longer, stronger, and equipped with a set of different sort of muscles so that they could move in ways arms can't. The itch was still there. It felt like it was inside my backbone where the bones of my wings joined my spine. It made me want to flex the long muscles that joined the wing-bones to the backbones. That's what I did. Doing that made me want to trot. It triggered something in my stubby little legs. Another kind of itch. I kicked and scrabbled against the asphalt of the parking lot and flexed my long arms. My long arms filled with air, like sails. Before I knew what was happening, I was flying. Over car tops, over the sidewalk, out across the street and its traffic. It took my breath away. I lit on a billboard advertising sinus tablets. Sadass joined me there.

"Son of a bitch!" says Sadass. "Isn't this hog heaven? Damn me if I ever want to be wingless again!"

It sounded basically dumb, coming from a genie, who could fly without wings if he wanted to, but I understood what he meant anyway, for it is a feeling as close to pure joy as I'll ever hope to have again.

I had my keen eyes on sheer blue distance. I hopped off the billboard and flexed the long muscles in my wings. Two easy flaps and I had more speed than the traffic on the street below me. Two more flaps and I had climbed the air a hundred feet. You can't know how easy it was unless you've been a vulture yourself, but I will tell you this: it was easier than walking and a lot more pleasurable. Sadass joined me and we headed west toward the mountains. Something in my vulture brain knew that the mountains was the place to go on a day like this. My fingers—well, I can't call them fingers, because they were feathers, but they felt like fingers—were harping the air, plucking tunes I could hear and understand, little hummings that told me truthful things about my speed and the direction and thickness of the wind, and by splaying these finger-feathers or by bringing them together or by turning them to meet the onrushing air at different angles, I could just about make any move I wanted to. Did it feel good? There aren't words, reader.

The mind is something that lives behind the brain.

I don't know exactly why I said that. Well, yes I do. You'd think that a buzzard's brain wasn't much more than a chicken's. And I guess that's true. So, having the brain of a buzzard—how could I still be me, a human being with all the complicated thoughts that a human being customarily has? I don't know. But I was. So, the only way to explain it is to bring in the mind, a separate thing that lives in, around, or behind the brain of the creature it governs. That make sense? Does to me. My mind felt the buzzard's brain, and it fit into it, like water in a hole. I knew what it was to be a buzzard, but I remembered what it was to be a man too.

We were way up there above the desert, I guess maybe nearly a mile high, when Sadass floats over to me and says, "Ulysses, I am half starved. How about you?"

"I could eat," I says. But I also had to admit that a chicken-fried steak or a platter of French fries sounded disgusting to me. Sadass slipped away from me then and starts a long circling downward glide. I followed him. I could tell he was looking at something way down below. Now my distance vision was always good. But these vulture eyes made my human eyes seem like the eyes of a potato by comparison. Even though we were thousands of feet up over the desert, I saw exactly what Sadass was looking at: a big jackrabbit that had been mashed by a car. It had been knocked off the highway into the barrow pit alongside and its belly had split from the impact. The red tangle of guts that spilled out from the torn meat made me hiss with hunger.

"After you, effendi," he says, as we drifted to an easy landing next to the big jack.

I didn't need to be asked twice. Damn if I wasn't the hungriest vulture under God's eyes. I waddled up to the big rabbit and breathed in his perfume. Now, judging from the condition of his innards and from the number of maggots wriggling in them, I figured he had been killed a few days ago. But his smell was more sweet to me than turkey in the oven on Christmas morning. I picked up a crusty red stringer of gut in my beak and gently pulled it free of the tangle. It went down easy and tasted like a combination of almonds and okra, only better. I took out several strings of that gut, and then Sadass stepped in to take his turn. He burrowed right in, sticking his whole head into the split belly. It looked kind of funny because, with his head gone inside to root around, the rabbit started to move, so that between Sadass and the jack they looked like a combination animal— rabbit and vulture. I laughed and out came a big belching hiss that made me jump straight up about a dozen feet. I was having a hell of a good time.

To a human the sky above seems like empty blue space, something that separates things with distance, but to a bird it is a thick and substantial thing that hugs and holds his body. Think of birds as fish and of the air as water, then you will get the idea of what I mean. The things humans make to fly all have to fight the air like an enemy, with the exception of blimps and balloons and gliders, which are at the mercy of the air and have no quickness. But the air is the vulture's servant.

We cleaned up the jack and then took off, heading west again.

"We were once worshipped by the Inca Indians," says Sadass. "They called us gods of the air. We're what they call condors, the biggest goddamned non-extinct flying animal known."

Below us, far below us, were the San Gabriel Mountains. You won't know what it is to feel good until you've been an old man with a worn-out pump who has been turned into a young condor. Think of the difference between scrub pine and redwood. Or dandelions and sunflowers. Tabby cats and Siberian tigers. Guppies and whales. A god of the air, that's what I was, where previously I had been a calcified piece of ambulating wreckage.

As we slipped over the mountains, barely needing to twitch our wings, I could see the brown smog piled high up on top of the coastal cities. It seemed next to impossible to picture millions of human beings living underneath that vaporized dung by choice. It might have been a depressing thought, but I felt too good to let it get me down. Just recollecting the memory of vulturing makes a sweet itch spring up deep in my backbone as though I still had wings there that longed to flap.

We headed southwest toward San Soledad where the upper air was a little cleaner. Far off to the northwest, I saw a couple of birds hovering over the green mountains of the coast. They must have been forty miles away or more, but with those keen eyes of mine they were easy to make out as condors. They saw us too, I could tell, and they were wondering why on earth we were headed southwest. Being curious birds by nature, they were thinking: What do those two birds think they are going to find to eat headed down *that* way? I was as sure of this as I would have been if they had hissed it into my ear in English. So I looked over at the highest one, wagged my finger-feathers at him, and confessed that we weren't really vultures at all but *people*, two-legged earth-bound killers of jackrabbits, having a little fun. For some reason this didn't interest that bird very much. He still wanted to know why we were headed in a southwest direction, since every bird knew the pickings were lean down there. What did we know that he didn't know? Then a crazy thought struck him: derailed freight train! Refrigerator car down in a ravine all splintered to hell and gone and spilling its cargo of freshly butchered cattle! It was a greedy thought and I replied to it by saying *no no*, over and over in my head, and he understood me, but was still skeptical of me, for a condor doesn't make purposeless trips anywhere.

"Why *are* we headed this way, Sadass?" I asked.

"Search me," he says. "I thought I was following you."

An idea had occurred to me a while back, but I didn't think I was going to follow up on it, yet here we were headed in the direction of that idea.

An idea will sometimes come into your head and you find yourself acting on it before you understand it's there or what it is. You know what I mean.

A while back, when we passed over that stretch of desert where the airliner went down, I thought again of Emily. Everything she had told me about Ansel Roe came back into my head. It didn't bother me this time, for I don't think there was anything on earth capable of bothering me short of having my wings clipped, but the condor's natural curiosity came into play and I all at once wanted to see this Ansel Roe for myself.

I peered into the layers of smog directly ahead of us and could make out the orange-growing country north of San Soledad. Home. It was about seventy miles away, but I could see orange dots scattered among the waxy green leaves. Home.

"You suppose he's still alive?" I says.

"Who?" But he knows who I mean.

"Ansel Roe. That wife-stealing son of a bitch who calls himself an artiste."

"That appears to be what we're on our way to find out," he says, adding quietly, "unfortunately."

"Appears to be," I says, ignoring his tone and flexing my big gray feet.

Today is magazine day. Holloway comes in from his trip to San Soledad loaded down with magazines. He dropped by with a bunch for me. "Here's one you might really like," he said. It's a local magazine published by a group calling itself The San Soledad Mysticone. What that's supposed to mean I don't know, and the magazine doesn't offer you a clue. This is one of Holloway's little jokes. The print is smeary and the paper feels like Kleenex. Here's something from the first article.

The life of the world is God's dream. What distinguishes God's dreaming from your dreaming is that God's is much superior and more cleverly detailed. The plight of the dreamed is that they cannot wake up. For a dreamed entity has no existence of its own. We call this "the human dilemma."

When God wakes, the world dies. We, the editors of Mysticone, have concluded that the world is beginning to peter out. In short, the great creator Himself is snapping out of his ten-billion-year sleep.

The most wide-awake of us are the most profoundly inexistent. This thought can be very unsettling.

Can the dreamed ever penetrate the

barriers of the dream? This is the sixty-four-dollar question.

Also, *Time, Argosy, Sports Afield.*

Ansel Roe's house was a little stucco box surrounded by runt palms. It was easy to pick out, being the only house in the vicinity of the Hungry Dolphin restaurant. There was a party going on in the patio. A bunch of people were standing around sipping wine and eating crackers. They were looking at a picture. I could tell all this from a couple of miles up. I figured Roe was the tall skinny goat-bearded one wearing a beret and sandals, although there were a couple of other possibles.

"I'm going down there," I says to Sadass.

"I'll watch from here," he says. "What are you going to do?"

"I don't know. Just look, I guess. I'm sort of curious about this artiste who steals other men's wives."

"You're going to scare the piss out of him, aren't you?"

"Don't plan to. I just want to have a good look at him, if that's all right with you." I guess I was feeling a little testy.

"Suits me," he says. "Watch your tail feathers, though. One of them old bohemians might be packing a gun."

Well, I didn't intend to flap down right in the middle of them. I figured I'd swoop down low from a half mile or so away, then light on top of the house, behind the chimney, which was plenty wide enough to hide even a big bird like me. If they noticed me, it wouldn't be until I'd had a good look at that old lizard. I wheeled around, let air spill through my wing feathers, and started a fast downward spiral that circled the bunch of phony-balonies in that patio. Then I swung away from his house and approached it low from the side opposite to the patio. I lit on the tile roof and walked across it to the chimney.

In the mishmash of voices I could hear one loud one saying, "Oh, Ansel! This is marvelous! The best party of the season!" I listened hard for the comeback, but it was swallowed in the chatter. They sounded like a cage full of goosey chimps. I peeked around the corner of the chimney. It looked to me like there were about twenty or thirty of them. There were some paintings propped up on easels, but more people were interested in the food Roe had put out than in the pictures on display, which I guessed were his. I don't blame them for choosing the food. The pictures were all the same— big waves crashing down on black rocks, and the white spray shooting up to form big sappy rainbows. Maybe he changed colors a little from picture to picture or here and there had a gull jumping up to avoid getting dunked, but they were generally the same uninteresting picture.

The tall goat-bearded one who I figured was Roe was talking to a white-haired woman he called Beth. Beth was dressed in a Mexican migrant worker's dungarees and denim work shirt, even though she had diamonds on her fingers big as grapes and was surely no Mexican farmhand. Their conversation seemed to be mainly about what a master painter Roe was. She was telling him how much she admired something called his ay-lan. She said the weight and power of natural forces in his pictures proved the reality of his personal ay-lan. Don't ask me what it means. Roe agreed with everything Beth told him about his pictures. He tugged at his goat beard and frowned and nodded to beat hell, like nothing truer was ever said. Roe looked about sixty, quite a bit younger than me, and younger by a few years than Emily. That burned me up and I was tempted to swoop down and knock him on his

bony ass, but I remembered that I told Sadass that I wasn't
going to do anything like that. Not that he would care one
way or the other, but I don't like to say one thing and then do
the opposite. Bear and forbear, like they say. It only makes
sense.

I guess you'd have to call him a good-looking man, especially if you are one to be persuaded by the surface of a
thing. But there was a shiftiness in his eyes, and an important
crinkling to his forehead common among people who fancy
themselves as indispensable additions to the world. Well, you
can hardly expect me to have liked the oily son of a bitch.
Still, at this point of my life, close to the end of it, the point
where you get an advantageous position on the unchangeable
past while waiting for the door to the unknown to pop open, I
didn't want to plague my mind with hostility and other back-
biting thoughts. Emily said her sin was spite, and I didn't
want to fall into that same trap.

Well, that was all high-minded and decent of me, you'll
have to admit, and I guess I felt sort of self-congratulatory
about it, but then something happened that made me forget
that I was a dying old man who had spent the majority of his
adult years talking to trees and reading long-range weather
forecasts. The thing that happened made me flex my talons
and spread out my wings. The old farmer known as Ulysses
Cinder was somewhere and someone else. I was a *condor*, by
God, and the thing that happened in Ansel Roe's patio
brought it home to me. Roe had gone inside his house with
Beth and when they came back outside he was carrying a big
picture of a woman. It was a life-size painting of Emily and
she was lying on a divan—naked as an egg! What was I
supposed to do? Sit up there behind that chimney like a mouse
when I owned a pair of ten-foot wings and feet like ice
tongs? Hah! The hell!

"Bucolic beauty," says Beth, reading the title which was engraved on a brass plate tacked to the wood frame.

"She was a farm girl," said Roe, "married to some clod from Kansas. Pretentious little wench, actually. She believed she was far above her *mari*, don't you know. She *was*, of course, but not as far above him as she liked to imagine. She was from Kansas, too."

"Oh, Ansel," says Beth, sort of scolding him in a flirty way. "You always were one for the milkmaids!"

Roe laughed. A dirty laugh, it was. He was a wheezer. "Indeed, *chéri*," he says. "And Emily here was a well-endowed milkmaid, don't you know. A veritable dairy farm in her own right."

"Ansel Roe!" says Beth, grabbing his arm and giving it a Western Union squeeze. His dirty talk had her sucking wind like a netted crappie. Even a simpleminded third party could see that Roe was interested purely in this woman's bank account. If you had good eyes like mine, you could have caught him flicking a lightning-quick glance at the stones on her chubby fingers every now and then. But all *she* could see was the hungry grin tucked in his beard, misunderstanding it for carnal desire. I wondered how much "shopping money" Emily had given this bilker. The look on Emily's face in the painting was one I recognized. It was a sort of dreamy look, one she often had while reading a book she especially liked. She'd look up from the pages, a million miles between her eyes and what they saw, probably imagining that she was one of the characters in her book. It always bothered me, for it made me feel lonely and left out of her thoughts. I was never one for books—oh, once in a while I'd pick one up—and I was surely never one for idle dreaming, and I guess that's exactly where I went wrong with Emily. And now, to see that look on her face again, made my condor blood boil. Did I say *I* went wrong? That's one for the books! I didn't go anywhere! She did all the damned going! Straight down to the beach house of this interloping artiste!

So I hopped off the tiles and spread all ten feet of wing, which made a big black shadow cross the party. All the pink upturned faces had little black O's in them. All eyes were snapping with fear. I just hovered there for a second, weightless, for I wanted them to get a good long look at what form vengeance from the sky can sometimes take. Beth dropped the paper plate that she had just loaded with cold cuts on her Mexican sandals. Roe was the first to raise up his hands to protect his face—double proof of his guilt—but I didn't go for him. Not yet. I swooped down into his guests, knocking plates and glasses out of their hands. I climbed up to a hundred feet, then came straight down and dug my talons into the picture of Emily and carried it down to the beach and out over the waves, where I let it drop. When I got back to the party, most of the people were gone. Their cars squealed away.

But Roe and Beth had slipped into the house. I saw the screen door whip shut behind them. I hit the door, talons first, and my weight carried me through it and into the kitchen. Beth, who had started to believe she was safe, let out a throaty roar that you would have believed was beyond the possibilities of the human voice box. Roe picked up a broom and started waving it in my face. "Shoo, you bad bird" is what he actually said.

"Shoo yourself, you goat-eyed son of a bitch," I says, but it comes out as a long hiss, like escaping steam.

Beth passed out. She hit the linoleum like a crate of produce, her nice white wig falling off, revealing a small pointy head that was almost hairless. Roe didn't even look at her to see if she was hurt bad. The only thing he cared about right now was the safety of number one—himself, the indispensable artiste. He gave a weak twitch of the broom in my direction. I jumped up and grabbed it out of his hands. But he was a quick thinker, I'll hand that much to him. He faked a grab at the broom handle, which was actually lying outside his reach, and then picked up a kitchen chair instead. Now, even to a condor, a heavy chrome chair is a formidable opponent. The trouble, though, was this: a condor just isn't afraid of anything. Oh, he will avoid a fight if possible, for he doesn't have any dumb notions that would lead him to think of himself as cock-of-the-walk, but challenge him on his own ground or airspace for what is rightfully his and you will have to contend with a pure fire-breathing force of nature with a bone-hard head big as a grapefruit, along with a claw-hammer beak and talons that make an eagle's foot resemble that of your back-yard robin redbreast. So the chair didn't scare me off. Of course it was *his* ground I was on and it was *his* airspace I was in, but there were other considerations, which I have already pointed out. It was a big, old-fashioned chrome dinette chair, and the muscle power behind it was skimpy and getting skimpier with each passing second of that confrontation. Then it began to wobble. Then it began to dip. He couldn't hold it up. As it dipped, his face came into view again. It was full of worry lines and the eyes were bleary and the thin mouth was downturned from the taxation of resources he just didn't have. He was an old man, like me, and probably no bigger a fool in the long run. Damn me if I didn't feel sorry for him. "You old sap," I says, meaning him, but also meaning me, and you too, if you fit the category. And then I turned and walked out of that kitchen.

I felt guilty and not a little stupid. People are people, and tomorrow will be another version of today, and vengeful condors aren't going to change those hopeless facts one bit. I also felt hungry. A condor, god of the air or not, has to eat a lot to maintain the gloss of his black-feathered glory. So I hopped up onto the patio table and loaded up on cold cuts and cheese. The bread and crackers didn't appeal to me. Then, after eating my fill, I packed my talons with meat for Sadass, who was still hovering overhead two miles up, and probably drooling, for I knew that he'd been watching the whole fiasco.

I'm cramped down here on the bottom of this page. Am I writing too small? This ends book 9.

*Here starts the tenth* and last of these notebooks.
Picnic day. We all packed up and went down to the beach.
Vi Honeycutt wore a little bathing suit. She pranced on down
to the water, Holloway following like a trained seal. I think
they have got something going. We stuffed ourselves with
potato salad and hot dogs. Someone brought a guitar and
someone else tried to sing. It was a nice day. Warm, clear.
Vi and Holloway were neck deep in water, letting the big
waves slam them around. I could tell that Holloway was
getting his hands on her whenever he had the excuse. There
were too many sand flies. The big event of the day was a
passing ship, a tanker. The old boys who had been to sea got
excited. Vi's top fell almost off. Holloway dove between her
legs, came up wearing seaweed on his head. I drank a lot.

Just for fun, Sadass and I toured the coastal mountains for
several days. We lived off mashed rabbits, dogs, cats, and
now and then a small deer. There aren't many condors left in
the world, so we had no real competition. The other scaven-
ger birds always gave us the right-of-way, except for the
crows and magpies, who wouldn't give the right-of-way to

man, machine, or beast. Two or three of them will scream foul language into your face while another pair pick out your tail feathers.

I guess I could have stayed a condor forever. I couldn't see a single reason why a man would want to be anything else. Sadass knew what he was doing, all right, when it came to knowing what happiness is. In the air I was perfect. I could see too much with my perfect eyes to ever get bored. Everything interested me: things that moved and things that didn't. My natural curiosity kept me alert. I began to understand something that I had always taken for granted as one of those unchangeable facts of life: that a man's life is spilling over with unnecessary worries. A man will spend his life in ten different kinds of harness and consider himself a failure because he didn't manage to get himself strapped into the eleventh. A man is purblind to everything God laid out in front of him. When Adam got evicted, God must have replaced his eyes with an inferior variety. I don't suppose all this is news to you, but if you were a condor for just five minutes those old sentiments would hit home with extra force. I suspect that if you were just a grub in a stump you'd get the same understanding of the unnecessity of most human enterprises. I don't mean to say things ought to be different than what they are. I'm just trying to describe the situation.

As a young man I would never have put down such feelings, for fear of being called an ass. But now I'm old, and you can call me what you want. By the time you are reading this, I will be under the sod. So what's the difference what I say?

There was some excitement in the air. It came to me as a kind of tingling in the ruff of lanceolate feathers that decorated the base of my neck. The tingling worked itself down into the skin, making me want to crane out my neck and turn my head this way and that. The source of it was the other condors in the area. It was also coming from other scavengers, birds and the four-legged kind.

"What's going on, Sadass?" I says.

"Big kill to the east," he says. "A lot of ripe meat on the ground, effendi."

"We going?"

"It's up to you. But I can't think of one reason why we shouldn't."

So we did. We turned east and followed our hunches. Pretty soon there were also a lot of other birds to follow. Practically all the condors from the coastal mountains were going there, along with smaller buzzards, such as the turkey, and of course the usual noisy crowd of crows and magpies. It was like we were on our way to a convention.

Ahead of us about a hundred miles, the air was freckled with hovering birds. They looked like gnats from that distance. We went up high to catch the swift winds that run west to east, and it only took us a little over an hour—judging from the changed length of the shadows below—to get there. It was the Grand Canyon. There had been a big kill of wild burros. The men who had done the killing were just getting into their helicopters to leave the area when we arrived. I didn't understand why all those pretty little burros had to be wiped out, but I figured there had to be a reason, since the helicopters had Department of the Interior insignias on them and the hunters were government agents. But reasons and explanations don't much matter to a condor. A condor will take life as it comes and not fret much over why things happen the way they do. As far as I could tell, there wasn't a single condor worrying about the sad fact that his kind of bird was nearly extinct. If there was only one condor left in the world, it would just go on being a condor in the way condors have always been condors—enjoying the sky and eating sweet carrion.

So I didn't give the helicopter hunters a second thought as I sailed down on the riddled carcass of a fine wild burro. It was still warm, but I didn't mind that too much. I preferred a little aging, but this would do just fine.

We stayed there for days, eating so much that we could barely get altitude when we wanted to fly. All the other condors were there too. There were less than a hundred of them, and most seemed to be females. They were good friendly birds with jolly dispositions. For such big creatures, their eating habits seemed overly delicate and polite. Once, while I was feeding on a speedily ripening burro, a small female lit next to me and waited while I pulled out a big rope of intestine through a baseball-size bullet hole. I backed away from the carcass with my prize and invited her in. She waited a little while, out of deference, then minced toward the burro with her big wings held out gingerly. I watched her dip her gray beak into the cavity. Her orange head, which seemed very beautiful to me, disappeared inside. She must have gotten excited by the treasure in there, for she quickly lost her timidity and pushed herself in all the way to her neck feathers. I stood back and watched.

Those wispy covert feathers under her tail were a pretty sight. I had what would be, by human standards, an impure thought. By condor standards, though, it was just another scent to follow up on. And so I mounted her. All it took was a little hop and I was on. She didn't back out of the burro and come at me with her claw-hammer beak, cussing a streak, nor did she hiss. She just kept on eating, as far as I could tell. I was careful with my talons, holding on to her with the underside of them—sort of like squeezing a rain barrel with the palms of your hands—and I had to keep my wings held out for balance. Mating with a female condor is like walking a slack wire while holding a live goose between your knees, but even so, I enjoyed it. I was probably going about it all wrong, but that didn't matter much, to either of us.

It was quick as a jolt of electricity and it seemed to make the interior of my head light up. When I hopped off, my head was still glowing on the inside. I had the notion that the light in my head was leaking out through my eyes and lighting up the landscape in peculiar patterns of all colors. The female was still busy inside the burro and I wondered if she had noticed the liberties I had taken on her backside and if the light inside her head was spilling out her eyes and illuminating the dark cavity where she was feeding.

"Sporting with the ladies, I see," says Sadass, lighting next to me.

"Couldn't see any reason why not to," I says. I could tell that he wanted to pull my leg some.

"Found a little lady myself," he says. "Got her exactly the same way you did, while she was satisfying her greed. Otherwise occupied, like they say."

"I don't see anything wrong with it," I says. "If you're a condor, you do things like a condor." But I wasn't at all sure if that's how condors did things. In fact, I was pretty sure it wasn't, but like I said, no one seemed to mind.

"Don't give it another thought, effendi," he says. "What you did is perfectly all right, believe me."

"I'm not giving it any thought. I know what I did was all right."

"Think of it this way. There is a real shortage of condors in the world. Now, the condors themselves don't have the foresight or interest to do anything about it. But as a human being, you *have* to care. That's what humans are for. So you should look at it as your sacred duty to help perpetuate this species of bird, and forget about the guilt aspect."

I knew he was pulling my leg, but I got a little burned up anyway. "I don't feel guilty about a damned thing!" I hissed.

"You see, as a concerned member of human society, you are obligated, it seems to me, to plow the socks off as many of these sweet little female condors as you are able to. And this burro kill sure has offered ample opportunity for that. So feel free, Ulysses, to save the condor."

"Why don't you go save a duck," I says.

Well, who knows? Maybe it was my mission in life. To bring back the condor, the god of the air. Maybe it was my duty, just like it was the duty of those government hunters to wipe out the wild-burro population. So I went back to work seriously. None of the other condors seemed to mind, males or females. Red organ meat had their full attention. If I wanted to hop females instead of hollowing out those fine burros, then that was my problem, not theirs.

I guess I hopped thirty before I lost interest. It was a good time. The light inside my head was blowing out through my eyes like wind and the whole Grand Canyon was filled to the brim with dry rainbows.

I lost track of time. There was day and night. First it would be day, then it would be night. When it was day's turn again, it seemed like it was the exact same day as the one before, coming back again through the front door after having gone out the back. The same was true of night. Same night, same day, coming and going, in turn. That's the simpleminded way a condor sees the passage of time. A short loop. It works the same way for seasons, only it's a longer loop. It took the arrival of men to establish the fact that yesterday is a lost cause and tomorrow is a second chance. When night came back, we slept on some big rocks near the tops of the mountains. When day came back again, we toured the strato-sphere. There was always plenty to eat and a whole lot more to see.

Then, while we were flying high above a coastal overcast, I blacked out. Dead faint. When I came to, I was falling like a brick. I had passed through the overcast and was nearly on the rocks that studded the shoreline before I managed to flex out my wings and glide to a safe landing. Sadass came down right next to me. My heart was fluttering like a trapped sparrow.

"What the hell was that?" I says, but I guess I had an inkling all right.

"It's starting."

"What's starting?" I guess I figured my fool questions would somehow put off the inevitable.

"Remember back in that Las Vegas motel I told you about the way a star will die?"

I remembered.

"Well, I'm coming down the backside of the final flare-up of my powers. We're at a place where all sorts of tricky shit is going to start hitting the fan. Like this blackout."

"Then, you are—"

"Dying."

There were some people a half mile away or so, walking up the beach toward us. They saw us, but they couldn't make out what we were. It was a couple, and the woman was telling the man that she thought she saw a pair of bodies fall out of the sky. I could hear them as if they were standing next to me. You'd expect a god of the air to have keen hearing, but this was more like ESP. The man told her we were seals and that nothing fell out of the sky. The woman said, "But I dis-tinctly saw two objects fall!" The man said, "You've got to cut down on those whites, Orchid."

"Dying?"

"Yes. And it will begin to happen very fast. As Ibn Al-Haitham pointed out, the increase in entropy, at the end, will be exponential."

"I don't understand what that means."

"It isn't important, Ulysses. Let me just say that within an hour I will be no more."

The woman was pointing at us and telling the man that we were not seals, for seals did not have wings, or orange heads, for that matter. They were still far off and were walking slower. It was early in the morning and there was no one else on the beach but us condors and those two people.

"What about me?" I says, but Sadass moved away from me, toward the surf.

"Is that all?" I says. "Is that all?" I guess I was squawking like a crow. It was embarrassing, but I couldn't help myself.

"I'm sorry, Ulysses," he says. "But the time of the Efrites is over and done with. Men, however long they last, will have to live without magic. Most men do anyway, so it doesn't matter much."

The two people had found a high perch right behind us, in the rocks. The woman was whispering at the man. She was telling him that we were a pair of angels. Fallen angels. She was wild-eyed and was crossing herself over and over. The man told her to cut it out, and that all we were was a pair of overgrown turkey buzzards that must have got disoriented in the heavy overcast.

I was depressed. I guess I knew down deep that I couldn't stay a condor forever, but having it all come to an end right there and then seemed unfair. Sadass had told me earlier that he was dying, but I guess I talked myself into believing it had nothing to do with me. But I was a condor for only as long as he was a genie.

"So you'd better prepare, Ulysses. You'd better give it some thought. I figure I can give you one big wish before I flicker out. So you'd better choose a good one."

"You mean I could stay a condor forever?" I got hopeful again.

"No. You can't stay anything forever. For a little while, maybe. But you'd revert back to yourself. Maybe you could stay a condor for a week, a month, even a year, but then it would be over. You wouldn't want to find yourself two miles over the desert when that happened, would you?"

Half the excitement of being a condor was in knowing that I was really a man. I don't think the ordinary condor had nearly as much fun as me. But if I became a full-time condor, who's to say I wouldn't soon forget what it felt like to be a man? In the few days I had been a condor, I had felt a definite slipping away of my human dispositions. I would have a human thought and I would have to look at it twice, for it would appear strange to me, even ridiculous. Now, let that process go on for a month, say, and I'd probably give up on the old human ways altogether. I'd be pure condor, through and through. Imagine the fix I'd be in when I returned to my usual form! I might be on the ground about to enjoy some ripe carrion when it happened. And there I'd be, a god of the air locked inside the body of a feeble old man, with no appetite at all for putrid meat. No, if I was to be Ulysses Cinder again —earthbound, opinionated, and almost burnt out—it had to be now. I didn't have a choice.

"I haven't asked you anything for myself, you know," I says.

"I know that. Not directly, at least. But now you must think of your future. It isn't much of a future, but you can make it a whole lot more comfortable and entertaining if you'll just give it some thought."

I thought. The two people in the rocks were getting excited. They were grabbing on to each other. Or the man was grabbing on to the woman, who appeared to be trying to jump off the rock. She didn't seem to understand that a thirty-foot drop would probably break her ankles, and he was trying to explain it to her. Both of them had gray hair that fell down in shaggy patches to their shoulders. "Whites," he said. "I hate it the way you gobble those whites, Orchid! Look at yourself!" She looked kind of birdlike, actually, and maybe she believed she could fly too. "Lucifer!" she screamed out at us, making the sign of the cross. "Lucifer!" just like she knew for sure that one of us was named that.

Well, I didn't know what to tell him. I guess I just wanted to live out the little time that was naturally alloted to me in peace and quiet. I wasn't dissatisfied with the way things turned out. I didn't even feel bad about Emily any more. People will be people. You want them perfect and you'll wind up goose-stepping through burning cities, changing no one for the better and a whole lot of others for the worst.

Death. I thought about that too. I was close to it. But it seemed a different thing to me now than it ever had before. It was like a magician's cape. Here's a rabbit, bub, presto, now it's a brown shoe. Changes. I didn't need to run away from changes, even if it was possible, and it looked like it wasn't even possible for genies.

The two in the rocks had started to clamber down. The woman was screaming some gibberish. The man was saying, "Shit, man," over and over, in a fed-up tone of voice, as if he had seen enough of Orchid's crazy displays to last him a lifetime. I figured they were just hippies who had outlived their best notions.

"You can't decide, is that it?" says Sadass. "Well, let me help you out, effendi."

There he was, telling me what my real wishes were again. But I didn't walk away.

"Let me say, first, that of all the masters I have served down through the centuries, you've been the best, Ulysses. I suppose it was written that the best would be the last. For even though my career is at an end, I feel no remorse, and I believe that this is due, in part at least, to your gentle, unselfish nature, effendi."

"Thanks," I says. And then we both spring up out of our condor bodies and are men again, standing in the cool sand, feeling the ocean wind stinging our human skin. The middle-aged hippie woman screamed and fell the rest of the way into the sand. The man climbed slowly down after her, but instead of seeing if she was all right, he took off down the beach like a rabbit with a dog nipping at its heels. The woman, who had gotten up on her knees, was staring wild-eyed at us and holding her arms up in a cross so as to ward off evil spells. I guess she figured she could be made, by some kind of evil magician, into something worse than she already was.

### To Vi Honeycutt, a special note

I guess if anyone is still reading this, it is you, Vi. So I wanted to tell you something. Just you. For I have come to like you a whole lot. You're an unselfish girl with a good disposition and a sense of humor. I guess you must have a lot of young bucks yodeling under your window.

I don't think you should read this next part, Vi, for I think it would be unsettling to you, even if you didn't fully believe it. There is always some small part of us that will believe a thing if someone actually comes out and says it. I think that no matter how civilized a man or woman is or how much education they might have had, there is always a child locked away and untouched by all our advances in learning. The dark still scares. Often, at twilight, deep in my grove, I would hear voices speaking languages few have heard. I have heard them laugh and sing. And there are beasts. I would do my work, whistling, but aware of a chill on the spine, and when I went back to the house, I would often fight an urge to trot. It's the child in us. The untouched one.

You might think: If he is so worried about me, why does he write?

That's a good question. I haven't got a good answer. I forgot why. At first I thought someone would find it interesting. Then I got involved in it, for myself. I wanted to see it put down. It's selfish. But then it was more than just selfishness. I couldn't stop. It was like a truck on a hill with the hand brake released. It picked up momentum. Nothing is going to stop it except the bottom of the hill, where it will either wreck or coast to a stop. I'm not even sure the driver is behind the wheel. You try to glimpse into the cab to see the driver, but there is only a shadow there.

So stop, Vi. Or go on, warned.


Sadass and I walked up the beach until we found a path that led up through the big rocks and on to the Pacific Highway. Some coincidence! Except I don't believe in coincidence any more. It seems we had come up from the beach in a spot that was directly across the highway from my old orange grove! I looked at Sadass—looking for the grin—but I didn't see a thing in his face.

"Sadass, there's my old orange grove, right across the highway," I says, but the look on his face is faraway and indifferent.

"Is that a fact?" he says.

There wasn't much traffic on the highway, it being early yet, and so we crossed it and entered the grove, which was miserably rundown. I had sold it at a better than average price seven years ago to a land developer named Kyle Sharkey, but he hadn't done a thing with it yet. Still waiting, I guess, for the price of real estate to top out. In the meantime, no one had been taking care of the trees. They were loaded with fruit and the ground was littered with old and rotting citrus in a stinking mulch of dry leaves. The trees hadn't been pruned at all and were thick with green suckers. They looked terrible. They felt terrible. I hated to see it.

I all at once remembered something I should have mentioned before this. Funny how something important to you will sometimes go unsaid as if it was common knowledge, even among strangers. I guess being there in the grove again brought it back to me. It was something that happened to Emily and me years and years ago.

Emily had come out to the grove with me to look at the crop. This was before she lost interest in it altogether. It was late in the afternoon and nearly dark under the trees. It smelled like rain, a salty warm smell that you first notice in your throat as a pinching in. There was some light, but it didn't seem as though it was light from the sky. It traveled flat along the ground, splitting itself through the trees and making the oranges glow like amber bulbs. This is what I mean about the grove. It's always different in there among those trees, from one time to the next, even hour to hour. If there is a wind, you will hear voices. If there is no wind, you will hear a solitary word every now and then spoken in a mumble, close by. Sometimes it will make you wheel around. The trees will loom or they will hiss or they will dance. All in twelve shades of green. No matter what your original inclinations were, once you start working a grove you find yourself talking to the trees as if your words could slip into the bark, drill into the heart, and run with the sap to the high branches and out to the leaves themselves. It seems the natural thing to do. To spend time in there without saying a word is hard. You'd have to be a fiercely preoccupied man to do it.

Anyway, Emily and I went out to look over the crop. It was close to picking time. It was one of the few times she came out there with me, and I was pleased. We went into the middle of the grove. You couldn't see the house from where we were. There was no wind. But now and then I could hear a lonely word or two. This is the sound of the grove. I looked at Emily to see if she heard it. She looked worried. She seemed a little uneasy. That will happen to you among trees in a dying light.

I said, "This rain, if it's going to be rain, is about two months late."

"It's a fine crop," she said. But there was something on her mind. It wasn't oranges she wanted to talk about, though she reached up and held one as if to inspect it.

I said, "Look at this tree here. It's old. Look at the bark."

She walked away from the old tree before I could point out to her the quality of the oranges it held. With her back to me she said, "Ulysses, there's something I've got to discuss with you."

I knew it wasn't oranges. Maybe I knew more than I wanted to know. More than I wanted to face. The blindest fool will get a feeling that things aren't right.

When was this? We were young. Relatively speaking. We'd had the grove some years by then.

1954 seems about right.

I walked up behind her and put my hand on her shoulder. The wind, starting in the west end of the grove, came up and made voices rise to a busy gabble, though the air where we were standing was completely still. Emily turned around. Her face was wet with tears and her eyes were wide, almost as if she was afraid. But it wasn't fear. It was like she needed to see everything at once, right away, all of it. Her lip was trembling. She tried to say my name but only sobbed. I swallowed. I don't think that if something had occurred to me to say just then I could have said it. I felt weak of knee and dizzy. We sank into the mulch on our knees. Something was trying to break loose in my chest. I held it back, for I knew it would be a groan or a sob if I didn't. We were kneeling there in the warm earth face-to-face, holding hands. It was as if our bodies were made of light. That make sense? I never felt a love like that for Emily or anyone else in the world before or since. I guess it was love. It was a maximum of something. I could have cut my heart out and laid it in her lap. She looked like she was going to die of a similar sentiment.

I saw her eyelids flutter, and her eyes rolled back, showing the whites, and her face seemed like it was carved out of white soap and I didn't know who she was. She fainted then and slumped against me. I held her tight, shaking like a leaf myself. She was breathing fast and her heart was beating high and light, like a bird's, and the voices were all around me, and the world outside the grove wasn't the world. Then I heard a terrible ragged sound. It was up in the trees, and beyond them, rising up into the low sky. It was me, a grating sound, like timber being ripped, as if a tree could feel pain.

What hit us? You'll have to ask the experts.

Anyway, the warm rain came then and brought us to ourselves, and we made love like we never did before or after, right out there in the open, in the rain, under the blowing trees, for it seemed required.

There were a few minutes of confusion, afterwards, as you might imagine. Neither one of us had any idea of what had

happened. It was a little embarrassing. We straightened ourselves up and walked back to the house.

I said, "We'll need to hire some Mexicans pretty soon," but
that's not what I meant to say. I said, "What was that you
wanted to talk about before . . . before . . ." And that wasn't it,
either.

"Nothing," she said. "Nothing important." And that was the
biggest lie of her life. Then she said, "That bell. Did you hear
that bell?"

I'd heard a few things. No bell. I shrugged.

She said, "Low. A rumble. Like stones falling on stones."

"I didn't hear anything," I said, for I was suddenly filled
with gloom.

Sadass and I walked up to the house. It used to be a nice
bungalow, two bedrooms, kitchen, living room with a stone
fireplace, an old-fashioned pantry, and a screened-in porch
that looked out on the ocean. It was all boarded up. There
was a sign: "Keep Out—This Means You. Trespassers Will Be
Prosecuted!—Kyle Sharkey and Associates, Inc." Another sign
said: "Future Site of Sunrise Haciendas—Elegant Homes for
Elegant Living!" The signs were riddled with dents from
beebee rifles.

The house was in bad shape. The shingles were half off, the
stucco had big, wide, foundation-to-eaves cracks in it, and it
was nearly covered with vines, out-of-control bougainvillaea.

"Shit," I says, for it was as depressing as viewing your own
corpse, unattended and moldering.

I tried to peek into a window through a crack in the
boards, but I couldn't see much since it was so dark inside,
but then I didn't try very hard either, for I was afraid I might
see Emily's ghost in there moping around among the cob-

webs. I had to sit down on the porch, for a stab of pain shot up from my chest to my jaw, so deep was it that even my tongue ached. I cleared my mind of sour thoughts and tried to take deep regular breaths. If nothing else, I persist in hanging on, almost a habit.

"Your time is getting short, old-timer," says Sadass. He put his big hand on my shoulder.

"I know it." I'd have been a fool to think otherwise.

"Have you come to a decision, my friend?"

Him calling me friend choked me up. I guess I was and am more senile than not. Vi, you can throw in with those of them around here who claim that the blood vessels in my brain have been clogged with calcium for years, and I won't blame you a bit. In fact, if you went ahead and read this far against my warning, you probably *should* throw in with them, for your own sake. Like they say,

> Peace of mind though built on lies
> is still peace of mind.

And in this life you take comfort wherever you can.

"I've decided," I says.

"Then quickly now, my friend. I feel there are only minutes of real power left to me. Then it will be done."

My mind started to race ahead. "I don't want anything fancy. Nothing more than any other human being has the right to expect. A simple thing, common, ordinary, decent—"

"Hurry, hurry—"

"Hold off. I'm getting to it. I do want something from you, but see, it isn't anything I couldn't get for myself, given a little more time and energy. You see? It's just that, well—" I didn't know exactly how to put it. I hadn't asked him to do anything for *me*, at least directly, and I understood this now to be a fault, a failure to recognize what he was, beyond a magical, seven-and-a-half-foot-tall Efrite—a *friend*. To let him do something for me now would be an act of friendship, something we both needed. I liked him and I think he liked me. I hadn't abused the gift he offered, but then I hadn't used it either. If you have ever offered a valued thing to another human being and had it refused, then you understand the kind of hurt this genie must have felt, considering the awesome worth of what he had to give.

"Ask, effendi, ask." He was pleading. It embarrassed me. I felt ashamed.

"All right, Sadass. Listen up. See this dilapidated grove of orange trees, and this rundown house? Take it out of here. Clean it off the face of the earth. I don't want to see a twig left, or a chunk of mortar. I want it *off*."

"I hear and obey on the head and the eye, effendi," he says, salaaming. We stepped away from the house. Then, quick as a tic, it's done. All of it is gone. Even the weeds. Nothing left but virgin brown dirt, twelve point seven acres of it.

"Okay. Now here's what you can do for me. I want a home for old folks. Not too big or fancy, but clean and well built. Let's say it's a home for retired businessmen, farmers, seamen, and skilled machine operators. That sort. No blowhards. Let's give it a name. Let's call it Sunset Haciendas—let's say this Kyle Sharkey sold the land to someone called Weldon Holloway—I had a great-uncle named that—he died in an iron-ore mine in northern Wisconsin—and let's give it a full staff of employees, nothing unusual, just average sorts. Okay? Let's have a paved access road that hooks up to the highway, a nice lawn, and well-tended shrubbery."

"Done," says Sadass, not moving a muscle. The smell of

fresh-laid asphalt hit me. It was all there, just as it is now, clean, cheerful, busy.

Get a grip on yourself. Vi, I mean. Vi.

I was trying to think of details, anything I might have left out.

"You will need an excellent nurse, to make your last days as comfortable as possible," says Sadass.

Stop reading now, Vi. Double your knowledge, double your grief, like they say.

But if you're stubborn, then consider this: calamity can be a friend in disguise. You might have even heard some say: if the sky falls, we will catch larks.

Cheer up, have a drink, and remember that I am the one that's dead and buried, not you. That's a lark of sorts, isn't it? It is.

"Yes," I says. I had a quick vision of my mother, Willa Tarmigan Benson, her warm arms holding me, her smile, the rocking of her chair, me just a babe, her singing voice. I gave in to the vision, which was a temptation. "Yes," I says again. "A nurse." A nurse to lead me into the birth of my death, like a mother bringing forth a child from the darkness of herself. I thought about this nurse. I described her to Sadass. A version of Willa Benson, I guess. Young, healthy, strong. "You think you can do it?"

"Yes, effendi. However, it will be the last thing I can do for you, for the end is very near."

You will fade, Vi. This is the calamity. Holloway will fade, the staff will fade, the old boys will fade, the building will fade. All will fade, Vi.

But it is only a *fade*. No pain, no fear, no lingering disease.

"Then let it happen, Sadass," I says. "Let her be a nurse called Vi Honeycutt, a name I've always liked, though I can't remember where I first heard it or who it belonged to."

And there you were, remember? Strolling toward us, talking to the old men who were taking the morning air.

"One thing, though, before you go, Sadass," I says. "These people here will eventually come into contact with other people. Now we can't have that, can we? Innocent people could get hurt if that was to happen. You see what I mean?"

"Put yourself at ease, my friend. I will see to it that there is no possibility for real interaction."

"How?"

You were about fifty feet from us, Vi, but you weren't looking at us yet. You were dressed in white—white shoes, white stockings, the perfect nurse. An eighty-year-old sea captain brought you a flower. You took it, put it in your hair. Your smell made him dizzy. He almost fell.

"No one will be damaged by the introduction of these new people into the world, for all the people that they will come into contact with shall themselves be images fashioned from available dreams."

"Fashioned from *what*?"

"From the subsoil of the present visible world, Ulysses."

I didn't get it, but he had his old sly look, it was directed straight at me, and I didn't have any notion of going further with my questions.

And so, Vi, it was done. Out of nowhere they came. The whole works. Everyone. And you. You were about twenty feet from me when you looked up. You were just about to ask me if I wanted bran cereal instead of poached eggs. I could see Holloway sitting in his office looking out the window at you, his tongue hanging out. Sadass had wit, he did.

"Good morning, Mr. Cinder," you said, your first words to me.

"Good morning, Vi," I said.

"Bowels moved yet?"

"Nope. Plugged tight."

"Then will you have the bran this morning, instead of the poached eggs?"

You touched my shoulder. Your hand was warm. You smiled. I felt weak as a baby.

I turned to Sadass to introduce him to you as a Mexican who used to work for me, but he was gone. Where he had been standing there was a lump of coal, about the size of a walnut. It was smoking a little. I bent down to it and touched it. It was warm. I picked it up and put it into my shirt pocket. Remember now? Then you went off to talk to someone else.

I went to my room, where I got a fit of the giggles. Some-one passed by and looked in. I heard the word "senile." It was a word I would hear often in the next few months. But I kept laughing. I laughed so hard for so long that I began to think that all the vessels in my head were going to unstitch themselves. I took that piece of warm charcoal out of my pocket and put it on my dresser. Now it was even smaller, the size of a pea.

Then I looked in the dresser drawers. They were loaded with good California wine. "Thank you, my friend," I said. I opened one and took a drink. It was better than I'd tasted in years. I proceeded to get very drunk.

So that's my story, Vi. It's your story too. But cheer up. Remember, you're alive and I am dead. So who is this joke on, anyway? You think, you feel, you move around. That means you are the genuine article, in my book. If it doesn't in yours, well, then try to think of it this way: when an orange is ripe, it falls. You didn't have any choice in all of this. If an orange could choose, it would make itself as hard as a stain-less-steel ball bearing and yet as light as the air. But it can't. I can't either. Sure as water runs downhill, an orange will fall, get peeled, and something will eat it. But you don't want to hear any more of this babble. I am drunk right now, once again, I admit. But like they say,

*In wine there is truth.*

I N T E R O F F I C E   M E M O
T O :   *Vi*
F R O M :   *Weldon*
R E :   *The Incinerator*

Kill *me*? Vi, I'm as indestructible as a pig-iron Dixie cup. Nothing's going to kill me except the sheer vapors of occupational boredom. Goddamn it all but I am up to here with these old bed-rats, your scribbling Mr. Cinder included. Amused? You think I should be amused by these senile peregrinations? Wrong, Nurse Honeycutt.

Look, Vi, you can't be giving Rita all this unauthorized work. That's my job. You can't abuse your position. That's my job. (Ha ha.) Seriously, I'm a little put out about this. Say, you just might have to pay the piper! I'll bet it took Rita all of three days to type it up, maybe four. Gee whiz, Vi, try to use your head. Of course I didn't read the dumb thing. It's a waste. It's what's known in the industry as steaming dogshit. Sure, I read some of it, the pickle business, the Jell-O. (You got some tricks I don't know about, you big devil?) I skimmed a few pages here and there. But listen, Nurse, there's nothing funny in the yuk-yuk sense about a worm-eaten brain. This is tragedy! You ought to try to nurture a little respect for the lame of body and foggy of mind. Decency must be our middle name, in this business.

And you send me this little pile of paper and expect me to read it with some pleasure. Nurse, I am sending it to the incinerator, where it belongs. Burn it, like we burn their poopy sheets.

There's a bug on my desk. One of those beetles looking for the orange trees that used to grow here. Even the bugs are senile. It's the atmosphere. You hear the one about the old whore who lubricated with Poly-Grip? I told that one to Mr. Carpel this morning, but he was dead. Lord, I am entertaining corpses, Vi. It has come to that. He was smiling pleasantly. I thought he was amused. But he was stone. He was dead. Mash! I just flattened the bug. It was staring at me like it recognized a long-lost friend. Wagging its big ugly blue head. As if to ask directions to the nearest orange tree. The bug stinks. It's the death stink, Vi Honeycutt. Of which I am weary.

Tonight? You better believe tonight! We'll do "Spies." But this time *I'll* ask the questions! Or maybe "Hijackers"? Think about it.